The Fierce
Are Fading

Joshua Daniel Howell

To Nicolai
NYCC16 !

The Fierce Are Fading is a work of fiction. Names, characters, places, and incidents either are the product of the author's imagination or are used fictitiously. Any resemblance to actual persons, living or dead, events, or locales is entirely coincidental.

Published by Fierce Literature
Fierce Literature is a registered Trade Name.

Joshuadhowell.com

Book design by Joshua D. Howell

To my wife, Maddie. Thank you for your support and care while I locked myself away to finish this.

CONTENTS

1 SEX, DRUGS AND MEAT LOCKERS

Seattle

The very first thing that Jessica Davis noticed about Todd's van was not the blacked out windows, not the tattered Nirvana poster, and not the twin bed mattress lying on the floor; it was the smell. Jessica couldn't deny that Todd was "cool", especially since he was one of the few boys at school with a car that wasn't furnished by a rich set of parents. Coolness, however, did not seem to hold a candle to the overwhelming stench of fast food wrappers and weed. Todd did seem to notice the abrupt change of expression when Jessica entered the van, and immediately apologized while reaching for a bottle of foo-foo spray. As Todd coated the van with the contents of the lavender-scented spray bottle, Jessica turned to wave goodbye to her friends who had dropped her off.

"Good luck Jessica!"

"We want details tomorrow!"

Jessica suddenly was a bit unsure as to whether she actually wanted to remain with Todd for the evening. It started as a dare between her friends, but had now blossomed into being dropped off in a Taco Bell parking lot at 2:30 in the morning with the hopes of losing her v-card to one of the "cool kids". Todd was nice at least. He wasn't a jock, but he was smart, kind, and he sold weed; only that last bit made him definitely part of the popular crowd. She did like him, but she doubted this would result in any kind of a relationship. Still, there were expectations to keep, and those brought her to this point.

"So, are we going to go somewhere?" Not that she wanted to go for a drive, but a parking lot wasn't necessarily the most romantic of places.

"I thought we'd stay here, and then I'll drive you home later." Todd chuckled as he lit a joint. "It's okay to be nervous. Would you like a hit to calm you down?"

"Uh…maybe." Before Jessica could reach out and grab the joint, the van suddenly rattled with a loud knock on the side door.

"Crap! Please don't be the cops, please don't be the cops!" Todd tossed the joint under one of the front seats, as if the smell alone wasn't enough to convict, and slid open the door. Outside stood a tall man, who had parked his red pickup beside the van. "Uh … who the hell are you, dude?"

"Wait, Todd, I know him. Mr. Jensen, right? Didn't you substitute for our math teacher last week?" Jessica was almost relieved to delay the night's proceedings, but then realized the overall creepiness of the situation and started to move back deeper into the van.

"Oh, right, Mr. Jensen. Hey, man. You're kind of interrupting something here so…" Before Todd could speak another word, the man now identified as Mr. Jensen grabbed Todd by the throat and threw him out of the van.

Todd hit the pavement hard as he heard Jessica's screams behind him. While he didn't look to be much of a formidable adversary to any degree, he righted himself and jumped on top of Mr. Jensen's turned back. Todd attempted a chokehold, the round the neck squeeze from every other action movie, but it didn't seem to work. Mr. Jensen reached up and grabbed the back of Todd's collar and sent him flying into the grass. With the wind knocked out of him, Todd struggled to make it to his knees before he looked up to see Jensen standing over him. Todd saw the gun in Jensen's hand and immediately put his hands out in surrender. All the while, Jessica sat frozen in the back corner of Todd's van. Even when she saw the gun go off, and Todd's body go limp in the grass, she couldn't force herself to move. Soon enough, Mr. Jensen returned to the van and began to crawl towards her.

****

The first body was found under the jungle gym at Green Lake Park; a sixteen-year-old girl who had been missing for three days. The second girl, same age, was found two days after her abduction, piled in a heap on the basketball court at Leschi Park. In both cases, the remains were identical. Each limb, and every digit, sliced and severed. Both bodies in their entirety were riddled with puncture wounds which ranged in size from needle point to the width of a dime. The cause of the wounds could not be determined as whatever made them appeared to have protruded from the body instead of being projected inward. Other than their age, there seemed to be no identifiable connection or similarity between the two. After the third girl went missing, FBI Missing Persons and Serial Homicide stepped in to form a joint task force with the local police. In reality, they were there to call the shots of the investigation, which made the department feel like a crowded kitchen.

As Special Agent in Charge, Riley Harper found herself trapped in the confines of the media spotlight, day in and day out. Every press conference presented the same uphill battle as she attempted to conjure up any kind of good news to feed the reporters. Not only was she under strict orders to keep the public at ease, but also to paint the local police in the best light possible. This, of course, was far from an easy task, as most of the citizens of Seattle viewed the FBI involvement as a sign that the police couldn't do their job. The fact of the matter was that the captor was quite competent. He had managed to grab and dispose of each victim without being seen, and the FBI's presence did not keep him from continuing at an alarming pace. Two months and seven girls later, Riley was tired and annoyed. It had become apparent, at this point, that only a lucky break would give them any chance of ending this.

Riley didn't mind being temporarily assigned to Seattle. Being a floater within the FBI meant that she was always on the go. When a field office was overbooked, she would receive a temporary transfer to manage the case. She had few constants in her life. Her supervisor, Agent Fischer, remained the same, but she didn't consider that much of a comfort. She had sold her condo in Austin on the fact that she only saw it for a couple weeks out of the year. Save for a drunken uncle, she didn't have a family to miss. She kept a low profile on each assignment, and made it a point not to make friends but merely acquaintances. Most of the time she wouldn't remember a co-worker's name after a couple days of finishing an assignment, and so the pursuit of friendship seemed pointless to her. Her supervisor worried for her; always asking how she managed to get by without making a personal connection with anyone. The truth was, she did get lonely, but she found ways of getting past that—diving deeper into her work, and finding someone to sleep with.

The nature of the job didn't allow for much personal time, so Riley eventually adopted a routine of picking a suitable companion from the crop at the office. She knew it wasn't ideal to mix business with pleasure, but she never stayed in one place long enough to feel the repercussions. It usually wasn't too hard to find a willing and impressionable officer to fill the role. In this case, it was young P1 Peter Drake. Peter was fresh out of the Seattle Police academy, looking to make a name for himself. Riley knew he was keen enough to realize the potential for him to move up the food chain if he stuck close to her. He was smart enough to keep his mouth shut, and in return she would give him high praise and recognition when the job was done. To his credit, Peter wasn't like most of the men who had accepted this deal. Most cases involved the guy getting too close for her liking. In this case, Riley had actually developed an attraction in return. There was a certain attachment that felt more than friends with benefits; something that she hadn't felt in some time. She knew it wasn't a feeling she should continue to entertain and should have broken it off weeks ago, but the sex was cathartic and their arrangement convenient.

Riley hated sleep, or at least the dreaming part of it. Her dreams were vivid and always of the disturbing kind. She couldn't help but feel jealous of people who could wake up without remembering or knowing if they had dreamed during their slumber. She woke every time, alarmed and relieved; alarmed at the content, relieved to find it was a dream. At the age of thirty-three, she could honestly say that she had more horrible memories than good. Her occupation forced her to remember each and every gory detail and sick revelation of every case she had encountered. She associated her general lack of trust, lack of empathy, and lack of optimism with her inability to forget the things she had seen. So it was no surprise to her that it eventually developed in her dreams. Tonight was no different, which made her less irritated to be woken by the piercing screeches and blinding light of her phone.

"This is Agent Harper," her voice croaked as she answered the phone.

"I need you to come in, there's been another abduction." Sitting up on the edge of the bed, Riley flicked on the lamp. Police Chief Daniels wasn't known to be a night owl, so Riley knew he must have something. A groan rang out behind her, which she quickly silenced by ramming an elbow between the sheets. "We've got a description this time; some lucky punk survived a bullet. I'm calling for maximum deployment till we catch the prick."

"Yes, Chief. I can be there in fifteen."

"I need you to swing over and pick up your P1, I couldn't reach him."

She rolled her eyes. That was because his phone was in her kitchen and he was passed out in her bed.

"Yes sir, will do." She hung up the phone and walked to the bathroom. Another groan rang out as she flicked on the light switch. "Can it, Peter. Chief wants us to come in. There's been another abduction. So get up!"

She splashed some cold water on her face, and stared at herself in the mirror. At the ripe age of thirty-three Riley felt like she looked at least a decade older. Her red hair fell to her shoulders and desperately needed some attention. She splashed some more water over her face, attempting to getrid of the bags under her eyes. It was enough that her cheeks were riddled with freckles, a constant source of hilarious jokes in her school days, but she didn't need to show blatant signs of fatigue across her face. By the time her eyes focused on the mirror she could see Peter already pulling on his pants on the side of the bed; she had to admit, he was efficient. She took a swig of mouthwash and spit as she fought the temptation to jump into a quick hot shower. The chief's tone was still ringing in her head, so instead she headed for the closet.

"You don't think the chief knows about us, right?" Riley did her best to ignore Peter's paranoid rant as she buttoned her shirt. "I mean, I haven't told anyone. Nah, he couldn't know."

"I don't have time for your insecurities, Peter. Grab my keys and let's go."

Throwing on her suit jacket, Riley walked out of the bedroom and down the hallway to find Peter, in full patrol uniform, working the coffee pot. She smirked. She knew the kid didn't even like coffee.

"It's fine, Peter. We'll stop by that diner near the off-ramp."

Peter tossed her the keys as he abandoned the coffee maker and threw on his coat. The rain was cold as the two sprinted for her car on the curb. Almost in sync, Riley started the car and Peter worked the heat.

****

Like digging for the surface after being buried by an avalanche, Jessica desperately struggled to lift the weight of her eyelids. When she could finally open them, she found that she still couldn't see due to a thick wool sack that had been placed over her head. Her fatigue began to fade as her panic set in. Strapped to a wooden chair, her hands were tied behind her back, with her knees and ankles tied to the chair legs. After a moment or two of struggling, she sat defeated, cold, alone, and confused. She tried to speak but couldn't muster anything more than a whimper. It was only then that she heard something shuffle behind her and realized that she was not alone in the room.

"Hush now, Ms. Davis. You're on television." The deep voice came from behind her and echoed within the room. She heard a click, and then the television to her left came alive in the middle of a news report. The wool sack was pulled from her head, allowing Jessica to see herself on the screen.

"...as yet another abduction has taken place here in Seattle. Jessica Davis, age 17, was taken from a Taco Bell parking lot earlier this morning. The tip was brought to the police by a fellow student of Jessica's, who was rushed to the hospital with a gunshot wound. His condition is unknown at this time." Jessica used to despise the voice of the female newscaster from Channel Eight; she had always found that voice to be incredibly dull and monotone. Now she couldn't help but cling onto every word. "Moments ago, the Seattle Police Department, in cooperation with the FBI, issued an official statement naming Harold Jensen as the prime suspect in the kidnappings. Jensen has served briefly as a substitute teacher over the last few months within three of the local high schools. Jensen is reportedly driving a red pickup truck. If you have any information as to the whereabouts of Jessica Davis or Harold Jensen, we ask that you call the number at the bottom of your screen."

"That's enough of that." Harold turned off the television.

Jessica's neck ached so much that it was hard to move her head and see what Harold was doing behind her. Harold suddenly grabbed the back of her chair, making her whimper and close her eyes, as he turned her around. Jessica tried to believe that she'd be safe, so long as she kept her eyes closed. When she heard another whimper in the room, she decided she could no longer keep them closed. What she saw, however, only caused her to scream again.

Across the room was another girl, approximately the same age, hanging upside down by a rope from the ceiling. Jessica recognized her as a girl from the west part of town, who had gone missing a week or so ago. The girl seemed to be waking from her own inertia and began to cry once she realized she was still in the same nightmare. Harold was standing at a table, pressing the needle of syringe into a vial of dark liquid. The other girl followed Jessica's eyes until she too saw the syringe and began to scream through the gag tied around her face.

"What the hell is this," screamed Jessica, but Harold ignored her as he grabbed the hanging girl by her thick blonde hair and pulled her head up towards him. Jessica screamed, begging for him to stop, as Harold pressed the needle through the girl's left tear duct and injected the contents of the syringe. "What are you doing to her, dammit?"

"Shut your mouth, Jessica. You'll find out soon enough." Harold put down the syringe and grabbed a stop watch from the counter. He stepped back and watched the girl as she began to convulse. Only a couple minutes went by before the girl began to leak blood from her nose and mouth, eyes and ears. Her moans turned to rabid screeches of pain. Jessica matched her screams as she saw black thorns began to break through the surface all over the girl's body. The thorns varied in size and length, but seemed to burst from beneath every inch of the girl's skin. The girl's screams died down as she drowned in her own blood. The convulsing finally stopped, and Harold threw the stopwatch to the ground. Grabbing a knife, he cut the rope and sent the girl's bloodied body crashing to the floor. After staring at her for a moment, Harold turned and looked at Jessica.

"Perhaps you'll be different."

****

Since Riley didn't have to drive to the opposite side of town to pick up Peter, she had time to swing by a twenty-four-hour joint and grab something to wake her up. She couldn't stand the coffee at the department, and preferred a fruit cup over stale donuts. Once they got off the I-5 North, Riley brought the car to a halt outside a diner under the overpass. Peter ran inside to grab the order as Riley stretched out in the car. She didn't like being the last to show up to work, but with her apartment in Renton, it only took a minute to get into the city. Seeing that Peter was waiting in line with two other people, Riley stepped out for a cigarette and leaned against the car. It was a cold night in December, and the weatherman had predicted snow all week. Instead the city endured this cold rain off and on. Adjusting her coat, Riley looked at the wall of water and was thankful to be under the overpass.

Checking the diner again, Riley watched as Peter shrugged his shoulders as the line didn't seem to be moving. Riley returned her glance to the rain, and saw the outline of someone in the dark. At first she thought it was a jogger braving the weather. Then the figure fell, and she heard the scream of an elderly woman. Tossing the cigarette, she called for Peter. He must have seen it too as he was already out the door and running towards the woman, who was frantically trying to get to her feet. Her nightgown and slippers didn't help much in the rain. The woman must have been in her seventies, and was mumbling gibberish as Peter picked her up and carried her to the diner. As Peter sat the woman down in a booth, Riley had the kid at the cashier call for an ambulance.

"Oh, yes, please, please call the police," the elderly woman cried out between her coughs as she shivered under Peter's coat. Riley brought over a cup of coffee to the woman and sat down next to her.

"Can you tell me your name, Ma'am?"

"Mona." The woman smiled as she sipped her coffee.

"Nice to meet you, Mona. What are you doing up, this time of night?"

"Oh, I always watch my soaps at night, child. I haven't been able to sleep at night for some time now. Doctor says I have insomnia or something silly like that."

"Well, I'm Special Agent Harper and this is Officer Drake. Can you tell me why you need the police, ma'am?"

The woman started to cry as if she just now remembered what caused her to be out in the rain. "Oh, it was terrible. I heard something outside of my window, and it sounded like screaming. When I went to the window, I saw them in the alley. But my phone is broken and I couldn't call anyone for help!" The old woman broke down in tears as she struggled to focus.

"Who did you see, ma'am?" Riley asked as Peter took the phone from the cashier and talked to dispatch himself.

"I saw a man in the alley pulling this poor girl out of his truck, and she was just screaming and screaming. Oh, it was just horrible."

Riley shot up from the table and made her way for the door. The woman just kept on sobbing and rambling on.

"He was taking her into that old Wolhner's grocery store at the end of the block. I don't know what for, though. That place closed down years ago."

Peter thanked the woman and told her to wait for the police as he followed Riley to the car. Opening up her trunk, Riley grabbed a radio and called in their position to dispatch as she handed Peter a bulletproof vest. Riley brought up the mat and grabbed a case from underneath. Unlocking it, she grabbed a shotgun and tossed it over to Peter as he grabbed a box of shells and headed for the front of the car. After donning her vest and securing her sidearm, Riley jumped into the driver's seat and drove up the street to turn into the alley next to the woman's apartment.

"Unit seven to Base, we've got eyes on a red pickup with matching plates in an alley outside of the old Wolhner's Grocery on 88th and Fort. Request backup," Peter reported to dispatch as Riley cut the headlights and brought the car to a stop just behind the pickup. Peter exited the car and quickly took a position along the right side of the pickup, while Riley took the left. When they found the truck was empty, the two followed the left wall of the alley as they moved toward the far end. Crouching beside the brick wall, the two peered across the street at the abandoned grocery store.

The large glass windows along the front of the store had been boarded up a long time ago, so there was nothing they could see from outside. Peter pointed out that one of the front doors was standing slightly off from the others. It had probably been jimmied enough to allow access, but still serve its purpose. Riley figured they had between three and five minutes before backup would arrive. She could tell Peter was ready, but told him to wait for backup before making a move. Of course she didn't like waiting any more than he did, but there were procedures to uphold and too many variables for a two-man team.

Just as she thought things were under control, a muffled scream broke its way out from the store and through the rain. Riley shot a glance at Peter, and shook her head. She knew there would be hell to pay if they didn't wait for proper backup. Peter then turned and ran back down the alley to the car. Moments later he returned with the crowbar from her trunk and took position beside her.

"That was definitely a scream, Riley. We can't wait any longer." Peter was practically bouncing on the balls of his feet like a sprinter on blocks.

"We wait for backup, Officer Drake!" She hated the look of shock on Peter's face. She couldn't believe what she was saying either. She sighed and tried to reason with him. "A scream means she's alive, Peter."

"Yeah, well, if screams mean life, I'm not waiting around for them to stop, Agent Harper," he said with disdain. He sprinted across the street and took position by the front door.

Riley cursed under her breath and sprinted after him. Peering through the opening between the doors, Peter signaled the immediate area was clear. Riley gave him a silent countdown, and stood with her gun ready as Peter pried open the door and broke the lock. The first inside, Riley took cover behind the lane one cashier. Peter shut the door as quietly as possible and took to the next lane. The two rose to tactical stance in sync, Riley's Beretta and Peter's shotgun elevated and ready, and eased out of the casher lines and into the first available aisle. The store was just as hauntingly silent as it was utterly dark. Aisles of empty shelves stretched to the back of the store with no one in sight. Riley motioned with her penlight for Peter to look at the floor; a path of wet footprints led down the aisle toward to back. Peter took point and the two took a left at the end of the aisle and followed the footprints toward what appeared to be the former meat department.

They came to an immediate halt as a light shot across the store from a door behind the meat counter. Riley could hear the far whirring of a mobile generator running somewhere behind the door. Harold Jensen must have taken up shop in one of the meat freezers. Once again Peter took position and peered through the open crease of the door. He signaled that the hallway was clear and rose up as he passed through the opening. Riley heard a muffled sobbing from the meat locker halfway down the hall; Harold must have gagged the poor girl.

As they advanced down the hallway, Peter kept his weapon on the meat locker door while Riley kept her sight down the hall. It wasn't until a shadow passed across the doorway that they were sure where Harold was. With Riley on his heels, Peter crouched down by the edge of the opening and peeked in to see Harold pacing around the locker. The missing girl sat tied to a chair in the center, with a rag stuffed in her mouth. Peter's eyes then found another body lying in the corner. The figure was covered in dark black and blood thorns of some kind protruding from within the body like a porcupine. Blood was seeping from every pore and crevasse.

****

Taking a deep breath, Peter turned to Riley and signaled the target was in the far left corner. As Riley moved closer toward the door, the shard of glass beneath her boot sent a crunching sound rippling down the hallway. Riley winced at the sound as she saw Peter do the same and grip his shotgun almost in prayer that Harold hadn't heard it over his frantic pacing. Peter turned to peek into the room again and found his prayers were unanswered as Harold stood in the doorway seemingly larger than he had appeared just moments earlier. Before Peter could process his panic, Harold grabbed him and threw him down the hallway as if Peter weighed nothing more than a sack of flour. As Peter hit the floor hard and slid into the wall at the end of the hallway, Riley screamed for Harold to freeze. Riley could barely get a shot off before Harold swung his arm into her and sent her flying into the meat locker's wall. Harold started walking towards her. With her gun out of reach, Riley simply raised a hand and screamed at him.

"You hear those sirens, Harold?" Harold stopped and lifted his head at the faint, but distinct sounds coming from down the street. "They're coming for you, asshole!"

Peter gasped for air as he watched Harold back out of the meat locker and take flight towards an exit on the loading dock with a swiftness as uncanny as his strength.

"Riley!" Peter made it to his feet and ran to meat locker. By the time he arrived, Riley was untying the girl in the chair as she held her side in pain. Spanning the room, Peter saw a table that reminded him of a college science lab—syringes, vials, a microscope, blood slides, and charts of gibberish. Just as Riley ungagged the girl, Peter heard someone break down the front door to the store; the cavalry had arrived. As Peter reported their position over the radio, Riley jumped to her feet and was out the door in seconds.

"The girl's safe, Peter. Now let's get the bastard!"

The two broke through the exit door and out into the dark rainy alley. The loading dock opened to an empty backstreet and a few vacant warehouses. Searching the darkness, Riley spotted Harold running into the third warehouse not half a block down the alley with large windows along the side. As the alley filled with cops, Riley and Peter waved them over as they breached the warehouse door and began splitting off into teams by room. The first floor comprised a large open bay with a few abandoned cars and office chairs. Riley directed a handful of officers to cover the exits and create a perimeter as she and Peter led a group up the stairs.

With several more floors to search, the group of officers began to thin. Riley took the eighth floor, and Peter followed the last two officers to the ninth and final floor. They went room by room, as they progressed down the hallway. The male and female officer would cover each door as Peter kept his weapon fixed down the hall. The two would breach and clear, and then return to the hall. As the three of them reached the third door of many, Peter gave the signal, and the first officer kicked in the door. A shot rang out as the first officer caught a bullet to the chest. The second officer was then abruptly pulled into the room before the door slammed shut.

Peter reported their location into his radio as he broke through the door and into a large empty room with rotting wooden floors, tall cracked bay windows, and thick support pillars seemingly spread throughout the room at random. Suddenly the room was flooded with light as a helicopter swung around the outside of the building. It wasn't until his eyes adjusted that Peter noticed the room was filled with homeless families lining the walls and desperately trying to shield their eyes from the light. In the middle of the room stood Harold Jensen; one arm wrapped around the officer's neck. Harold had the officer's gun pressed against her temple as he tried to shield his massive figure behind her.

"Let her go, Harold! You've run out of options here," Peter screamed as he dropped the shotgun and trained his sidearm in Harold's direction. Even with Harold as large as he was, Peter couldn't find a clean shot without endangering his fellow officer in the process. She looked at him, helpless and ashamed to be in the situation to begin with. Peter didn't really know her, but it didn't matter. "Stop moving, Harold. I said stop moving!"

"I'm sorry ... he was too fast," the officer said as she choked for air beneath Harold's grip. Harold's face was unflinching, even as the blood flowed thick from a wound in his shoulder where Agent Harper must have caught him in the meat locker. Peter took a step forward and held his aim with both hands as he repeated his command. Harold took a step back and pressed the barrel of the gun harder to the officer's head.

"Drop the gun, or I will kill her. Simple," Harold said as he simply continued to drag the officer backward and away from Peter. Harold's solemn expression then suddenly changed to unease as his foot broke through a rotted floorboard and caused him to desperately tighten his grip as he stumbled backward. The officer's expression broke to despair in the last seconds as Harold's finger also tightened around the trigger and sent a bullet tunneling through her skull.

Peter screamed in protest as the officer went limp and fell to the side while Harold struggled to free his leg. Before Harold could make any progress, Peter pulled back on the trigger and sprayed Harold with two bullets to the chest and one to the center of his forehead. As Harold hit his knees with a thud and slouched back, a slew of officers made their way through the door. Agent Harper entered the room and saw Peter staring down in misery at the officer's body. She put a hand of Peter's shoulder.

****

As the officers worked the warehouse, Agent Harper waited in the alley for the chief to arrive on scene. She saw Jessica Davis being wheeled out on a stretcher toward an ambulance. Jessica met Riley's stare and winced as she raise a hand. Riley smiled and waved back; at least someone was saved tonight. Riley shifted her gaze toward the Escalade coming to a halt on the other side of the alley. Police Chief Daniels stepped out of the passenger side, and immediately landed in a deep puddle.

"Well, that's fantastic." Chief Daniels donned his peaked cap and met Agent Harper. "All right, I want to be caught up before the news crew arrives. Let's hear it."

"We recovered one girl alive, although she said she was injected with something. One officer down. Jensen caught her off guard, grabbed her gun and put one in her head. Another officer took a round to the vest, but he'll be all right. Officer Drake returned fire and put the prick down."

Chief Daniels sighed as he turned to see a gurney with a body bag being carried off to his left.

"Sounds like a mess, Agent. At least it was a cop who put him down." A news van came screeching to a halt, almost hitting a police cruiser behind the Police Chief. He sighed again and wiped the rain from his face before turning back to Agent Harper. "Well, at least you'll be leaving this hell hole soon. How's my tie?"

****

Once the room was cleared and the crime scene properly marked off, a few officers stayed behind to setup lights for the investigators. Slouched down at the base of a support pillar, Peter listened with disdain as a mixed group of commentators formed around Harold's body. Still upright on his knees with his head hanging back, Harold was apparently quite the spectacle. After everyone offered up their two cents, the spectating officers eventually dispersed and went about their way. Peter just stared at Harold, as if waiting for him to sit up straight and return his gaze.

Harold did just that, and Peter nearly toppled over at the sight.

While everyone else in the room was busy with something, Peter was apparently the only person who took note of Harold's silent and slow attempt to pull his leg out of the hole in the floor. Peter tried to form the words to alert the others, but he couldn't speak. Once Harold's leg was free, he simply stood up and began to pull his shirt up and over his head; blood still draining from the two holes in Harold's chest. Harold let out a light groan as he tugged the last of the shirt off, and suddenly everyone in the room was aware of the anomaly and raised their weapons.

Amid the shouting for Harold to get back on the floor with his hands behind his head, Peter couldn't help but notice that Harold was still staring right at him. Harold smiled as his right hand pressed against a large black circle tattoo along his ribcage. As something beneath the skin began to flash an eerie red light, Peter sprang to his feet and sprinted in Harold's direction.

"Bomb!"

It was the only thing Peter could think of. Something implanted under the skin could be enough to simply dissolve Harold from the inside out, or enough to disintegrate everything on this side of the building. Peter ran towards his enemy without hesitation, spreading his arms and motioning for everyone to clear out. Before he could think of a better idea, Peter tucked his head down low and tackled the massive center of Harold's looming figure. With all the strength and adrenaline he could muster, Peter took Harold through one of the cracked bay windows and out into the open air.

As if he were in the front seat of a rollercoaster, approaching the drop, Peter realized the fall ahead. The walls of the surrounding buildings were painted red and blue as the street below was filled with squad cars. He released Harold and reached out into the emptiness, as if expecting to suddenly have the ability to fly. He saw the Police Chief standing next to Agent Harper amongst the cars below. Finally, Peter looked down to see Harold just staring up at him, a half-surprised and half-content smile upon his face. Just before the ground caught up with the two of them, a bright parade of green light flooded the spectrum. Peter wondered if it was an expressway to the next lift, or an angel's hand covering his eyes at the last moment. Nonetheless, Peter ran out of room to fall and his body collided with Harold's and the cold, hard ground.

****

Agent Harper heard someone scream about a bomb, and turned to stare up at the windows of the warehouse's ninth floor. Without warning, the windows shattered as Officer Drake and Harold Jensen came crashing into the night air. Before she could yell for everyone to get clear, a bright green light, an explosion perhaps, projected outward from Harold's body. Riley closed her eyes and turned away from the brightness as she heard the bodies hit the ground behind her with a thud. She turned around to see the seared, severed bottom half of Harold's body lying on the ground before her in a puddle of blood. Unable to process what had just transpired, Riley simply fell to her knees and screamed.

"Peter!"

Joshua D. Howell

2 THE COLD WHITE DESERT

He could see her face, smiling back at him like she rarely did. The sun was rising, breaking in through the curtains, and running over the skin of her exposed shoulder. Perhaps they didn't need to leave this time. The clock was ticking, the day had arrived, but he didn't wish to move. He took her face in his hands and kissed her deeply. The texture of her lips could make him forget any obligation that could break him away from this place.

"I know what we agreed upon Riley, this arrangement of ours, but I don't know if I can keep up my end. I've been compromised."

She smiled, but didn't respond. Instead, she wrapped her arms and legs around him, making no effort to vacate the sheets beneath which they were currently lying. Atop him now, her hair fell down around his face as she returned his kiss.

"I think I slipped up and fell for you, Riley, and I'm not sure if I can undo that."

She said something to him, but Peter couldn't make it out. She had that smile though, blindingly beautiful, and he couldn't take his eyes off her. He felt like he shouldn't be there, with her in that place. It wasn't the first morning he had woken up next to her, but this morning felt different. It was certainly out of character for her not be out of bed and half-dressed by this point, but that wasn't what felt off. As he fought to enjoy the moment, to hold her body closer to his, to feel her skin against his, he couldn't get rid of a nagging feeling of despair in the back of his mind. Then clarity arrived, and he knew why he felt this way, why he shouldn't be there in that place with her.

"I dreamt I was dead," and with that the light began to fade, Riley's smile began to blur, and Peter slowly became more and more aware of the cold biting at his face.

****

Officer Peter Drake opened his eyes to find that he was in fact not lying next to Agent Harper, but was instead slouched in a seated position with his face against the cold steel wall of what appeared to be a vertical cylinder of some sort. He fought to adjust his eyes as he took in his surroundings. The room resembled a locker room, like in some fancy spa, with everything from the ceiling to the floor covered in chrome—the lockers, the sinks and showers, the steps that led up to the row of the vertical, open-faced cylinder in which Peter lay. As his eyesight focused a bit, Peter noticed the one blemish on the perfect silver of the floor; the top half of Harold Jensen's body lay on the steps before him, his insides leaking out the bottom of him.

"How the hell did I get here?" Looking up, Peter saw a sign on the walls above the cylinders. "Receiving Units? What the hell does that mean?"

Peter moved backward, deeper into the cylinder as he focused on the body. Within the stew of guts and innards, Peter saw what looked like a disc, flashing the same red light he had seen earlier in the abandoned warehouse. Peter reached out and grabbed the disc, the size of a salad plate, to get a closer look. As he tugged to free the disc, several tiny wires and tubing tore free from their attached veins and organs. There was nothing identifiable on the surface of the disc, but Peter could only assumed that his was the answer to how he ended up here and not on the pavement in that alley. Before he could manage another thought about his predicament, the entire room began to flash red, and a noise blasted over the intercom.

"Intruder alert! Intruder Alert! Unauthorized transport in Bay 2!"

Peter stumbled to his feet and scrambled to find a place to hide. Tip-toeing around the blood puddles, he resorted to cramming himself in one of the lockers and praying they didn't already know he was there, whoever "they" were. Within moments the double doors to the room burst open as a man and woman in lab coats entered, escorted by three or four armed guards in black tactical gear with tinted glass faceplates.

"Oh, what the hell is this?" The male scientist stood over Harold in disgust as his female counterpart crouched over the body. "Who is it?"

"Looks like one of our field assets teleported back to base. His disc looks fine, must have been overloaded somehow. Too much weight or something?" The female scientist brought the disk under some type of scanning device, as she sighed at the mess. "Odd. I wonder why he came in."

"Would someone please turn off that damn alarm!"

One of the guards tapped the side of his helmet and said "All clear," and the alarm ceased its blaring through the overhead speakers. The male scientist went on to examine the vertical cylinder as the female scientist read the report on her tablet uploaded from the device.

"The asset's name is Harold Jensen. He was assigned to Seattle as a part of our procurement and testing division. Apparently he went AWOL last month and hasn't reported in since."

The male scientist groaned as he accidentally stepped in the blood. "We'll need to notify the head office. Call it in and then get someone down here to clean this place up. Have them bring the body to the lab for further testing."

As the group left the locker room, Peter softly creaked open the locker door and stepped out. Wherever he was, he only had seconds to make a move before he would be discovered. Peeking his head out the door, Peter found himself in an empty corridor seeming to go on forever. As quietly as possible, he ran down the corridor, searching for an exit or some kind of sign as to where he could possibly be. Finally the corridor led to a large open room with a mural of the world map engraved into the marble wall.

Peter gazed at the map. Across it were red, blue, and yellow lighted dots, seemingly in every country across the planet. Engraved across the map, in large somber letters, were what Peter could only assume to be the name of the entity who controlled this facility, *M.O.R.S. Initiative*. Beneath the map was a bank of computers mounted to the wall, but after a couple brief keystrokes, Peter realized he had no way of getting past the login screens; he was a cop, not a computer hacker. Knowing his chances of getting caught grew with every second, Peter continued down the next corridor until he came to a junction. Peering around the corner, Peter found a set of elevators guarded by two armed men. Both guards wore the same black tactical suits with the faceless tinted helmets.

"I don't know what happened with Jensen, but he might've found a chosen one," one of the guards said.

"What? How do you know? He's dead!"

"Seattle News. One girl made it out of Jensen's capture alive and well."

"You saying she survived an injection? She's a match?"

"Certainly appears that way."

As interesting as this conversation was, Peter couldn't afford to listen to it anymore. As the guards turned their backs, Peter continue down the hall, desperately trying any door he could come across. Failure after failure, he continued down the hall, begging for a door to work.

"Come on. Open sesame..." Peter pleaded as he turned the handle to the next door. To his surprise, the door gave way and Peter found himself in a storeroom. On the back wall of the room, a metal ladder was mounted to the cement wall with a sign next to it reading *Emergency Exit Hatch*.

Peter climbed the ladder up what seemed like twenty or thirty stories, every second of which with the horrible feeling that someone was about to see him. He started feeling claustrophobic as the majority of the ladder was surrounded by a concrete tube, only breaking every few stories or so in random dark rooms. Finally, in the dark, Peter reached the top. He felt around for some kind of lever or knob. Eventually he found what felt like a valve wheel and started turning it, breaking away what felt like decades of rust as the wheel creaked loudly. Peter could only pray that he wasn't opening the door to something worse on the other side. Desperate to free himself from the dark surrounding him, he picked up his pace and press his shoulder against the hatch until it finally broke its seal and opened.

As Peter crawled out of the hatch, his aching

body collapsed on the cold ground. He squinted as the blindingly bright sun reflected off a vast white blur. He fought to overcome the longing to lie there and rest for a moment, but Peter knew his time was limited. As his eyes focused against the brightness, Peter found himself in the middle of a snow-covered corn field. Rising to his feet among the small brittle cornstalks, Peter scanned the horizon for any sign as to where he could be. Washington hadn't received this much snow in years, so he knew he couldn't be anywhere near Seattle. After seeing nothing but endless hills of snow, Peter picked a direction and began to jog, hoping he would find something in this cold white desert.

****

"Seattle can finally rest tonight, as the kidnapping spree has come to an end. Friends and families continue to mourn the loss of several young girls in the area, while others find comfort knowing that one lucky young woman survived this horrendous affair. Jessica Davis was released from the hospital this evening with a clean bill of health. Her parents have asked for privacy as they take their daughter home for care."

Riley struggled to listen to the television broadcast over the crowd at the bar as she downed another shot of Maker's Mark. The place was filled with off-duty cops paying tribute to their fallen comrade; not with drunken songs and shouts of victory, but testimonials and salutes. A large picture of Office Peter Drake, obviously a half-assed print off from Kinko's, was propped up on a table in the corner, surrounded by shots and glasses each filled with a variety of liquors.

Harper didn't feel all too welcomed by the group, as she was still the FBI outsider in the bunch. At the moment, however, she felt like the only one grieving. Sure, it wasn't her place to judge, but she didn't feel like singing or shouting at the moment. Instead, all she wanted to do was drown herself in whatever bottle she could find. She would have never admitted it to Peter, but she had cared for him, more than she usually cared for anyone. She felt silly to think of how out of control her emotions had become. This was not supposed to happen, no matter what the outcome of the case became.

The only comfort she could find was knowing that the girl was safe. Before she had left the crime scene, she had returned to the meat locker. She had seen the body of the other girl, brutally disfigured and covered from head to toe in dark sharp spikes, protruding from within. It was a sickening sight. Whatever Harold had injected her with, he also injected Jessica the same. She, however, seemed to not react to it, and that was the only victory of the night. Now Jessica could return home and try to sleep off the nightmare of the last twenty-four hours.

Riley, however, knew that sleep wouldn't let her escape her horrors. So she ordered another line of shots instead.

****

Peter finally found a footpath in the snow that led him to a road. When he saw no cars in sight, he decided not to wait, and resumed his jog down the road. He had no idea where he was, but he knew he wasn't safe. A facility like the one he just escaped from had to have some kind of surveillance. It wouldn't be long for them to find out he had been there, if they didn't know already. His only hope was to find a house, or, better yet, a car, so he could let someone know he was alive.

The sun bore down upon him. While the snow was nowhere close to melting, Peter felt like someone was holding a magnifying glass overhead, burning him to the core. He had to keep moving, but with every stride he took, he felt his aching body betray him. Sooner than later, his adrenaline was going to wear off, and he would fall and not be able to get back to his feet. Just as he was about to give, however, he saw something along the side of the road—a mailbox.

Peter opened the mailbox and grabbed a handful of the mail inside. He flipped over the envelopes, anxious and desperate to know just where in the hell he had ended up. The top of the first letter read an address that ended in North Bend, Nebraska. *Nebraska? That's not possible.* Peter raised his head to see a house down a private dirt road. The envelope had read that the residence belonged to a Mr. and Mrs. Jenkins. He dropped the mail and bolted down the dirt road. He was close to freedom, he knew it, and he wasn't about to give up yet.

"Hello? Anyone there? Mr. Jenkins? Anybody?" Peter banged his fist against the front door. He peered in through the windows, but couldn't see past the curtains. There wasn't a car in the driveway, and he didn't hear any movement inside. The longer he waited on the porch for a response, the more vulnerable he felt. He had to get inside.

Peter kicked in the door and quickly closed it behind him. He stayed there for a moment, leaning his weight against the door, waiting to hear any kind of movement within the house. When he heard nothing, he made his way to the back of the house. Peering through the windows, he saw no one in the backyard and figured they must have gone into town or something. He turned around and faced the kitchen. Before he could think of anything else, a sudden abrasive thirst overtook him and forced him to stumble over to the refrigerator in hopes of finding a cold drink inside.

The refrigerator was bare, save for half a loaf of banana bread and a bottle of milk. He grabbed both and stumbled back into the kitchen counter as he popped off the bottle's lid and began chugging it down. When he finally came up for air, Peter saw the house phone mounted to the wall near the hallway, and immediately reached for it. Of all the numbers he could call, of all the voices he could hear, he only longed for one.

****

Riley lay face down on her couch, with one hand hanging off the edge, clinging to a bottle of scotch. It was only late afternoon but she couldn't fight her need to rest. The alcohol and her sorrows had beaten her, and she wasn't willing to fight either of them anymore. She could feel herself sinking into that deep sleep, where the sounds of the city began to fade, and the whirring noise of the house fan flooded out her senses. Perhaps the alcohol would allow her to dream of happy things, but she knew that was too optimistic for her reality. Just as the bottle began to slip from her hand, her cellphone rang.

"Agent Harper." She could barely say her own name, but she brought the phone up to her ear and attempted to listen.

"Riley! It's me! Thank God you picked up!"

****

Riley shot up to a seated position, battling the alcohol and the sudden blood rush. She tried to convince herself that she had actually heard his voice.

"Peter!? Is that really you?"

"Yes, it's me. You won't believe where I am."

"How is this…? I thought you were dead! I saw you explode in that alley, I don't understand." She held her aching head as she subconsciously screamed at herself to stop talking so she could hear his voice again.

"I can't explain it either, Riley. But I'm alive, somehow, and I'm standing in a house in North Bend, Nebraska. 20433 Franklin Road."

"Nebraska? How is that possible?"

"I don't get it either, but I woke up in this place called M.O.R.S.. And then I…" He paused. Riley could hear him bumping into things. "I think there's someone here."

Riley heard a crash and glass breaking before the line went dead. She screamed in anger and quickly redialed the number on her phone. The phone rang once before she heard the auto-operator informing her that the line had been disconnected.

"We're sorry, but the phone number you dialed cannot be reached or is no longer in service."

She jumped to her feet, only to slip on the bottle of scotch and fall back to the couch. She let out a deep breath and collected herself. Now was not the time to lose her composure. She quickly dialed her handler and put the phone on speaker as she got dressed.

"This is Special Agent Riley Harper. SCID: alpha-six-delta-five-two. I need to speak to Agent Mike Fischer, and I also need a field unit sent out to 20433 Franklin Road in North Bend, Nebraska right away."

3 NOTHING LIKE LATE NIGHT T.V.

Omaha, Nebraska

Riley stormed down the hallway at the Omaha FBI building, passing several rows of cubicles, till she reached the secretary for her supervisor. The secretary, an elderly woman with a flowered dress and small curved glasses, sat there watching a cat video on her computer. Riley knew exactly who she was, as Agent Fischer seemed to take her everywhere he went. He outfit and demeanor defied any sense of professionalism. Riley cleared her throat, and the secretary groaned and gave Riley an annoyed glance.

"Yes, dear, is there something I can assist you with?" The secretary's tone was far from genuine.

"I'm Agent Harper, and I need to see Agent

Fischer immediately."

The secretary glanced at her phone and then back at Riley.

"Agent Fischer is on the phone right now, and he's got a busy afternoon. You'll have to come back later."

Riley stared down at the secretary, almost as if the two were engaged in a staring contest with both their lives on the line.

"The hell I will." Riley sidestepped the secretary's desk and headed straight for Agent Fischer's office. The secretary called after her, but it was too late. Riley burst through Agent Fischer's door just as he was hanging up his phone.

"Now what the hell is this, Harper? You trying to piss me off?"

"That's it? We're just going to call it? You've got to be joking here, boss." Riley paced back and forth inside the office.

"Harper, we've done all we can at this point, and frankly, we've wasted enough resources and man hours on this wild goose chase of yours. You need to face facts and let this go." Agent Fischer sat in his chair, elbows on his desk, hands running through his graying hair.

"Face the facts? I've given you the facts. Three days ago I received a call from Officer Drake during which he barely had time to tell me where he was and who was holding him captive." Riley slammed her fists down on the edge of Agent Fischer's desk. "Now I brought those facts to you, and you've given me jack shit in return!"

"Officer Drake is dead! He's dead, Riley!" Fischer rose from his desk, no longer able to listen to this nonsense. "You saw him get blown to smithereens in that alley in Seattle! Listen to yourself!"

"He's not dead. He can't be! He called me, dammit!"

Fischer sighed as he massaged his sinuses.

"You're really going to make me do this, aren't you?" He sigh once more and then walked past Riley to shut the door to his office. "You screwed up, Harper! You were supposed to crack the case, but you let it run on for far too long. In the end we got dead cops, dead girls, and where were you? You were shacking up with some rookie fresh out of the academy. Now you're in here slinging some delusional shit about him being alive here in Nebraska? There's no record of any call on your phone coming from this state. There's no record of any outgoing call from the address you gave us, and no one lives in that house but an elderly couple on their way out. Now I've entertained your guilt for three days. Our agents found nothing, absolutely nothing, to suggest that Officer Drake was ever in that house. So don't tell me I didn't do my due diligence."

"But I don't understand, boss…"

"I do, Harper. You're tired. We've had you out and about as our floater for too long. You've lost your edge." Agent Fischer turned away from her and peered out the window. "You need rest, a break from all this. So I'm putting you on paid leave for a while."

Riley stood there in shock. Was this really happening to her? She had booked it to Nebraska to find her partner, and now she was being told that none of it happened. On top of that, her boss was suspending her. This couldn't be happening. Unsure what to say, she removed her sidearm from her shoulder holster and set it down on the desk, along with her badge. Fischer heard this and quickly turned around with his hands in the air.

"Oh, enough with the drama. I don't want your badge. I'm not firing you. I'm not even officially suspending you. I just want you to go somewhere for a while. Rent a car and go sightseeing or something."

"For how long?" Riley couldn't think of taking a vacation. Not now. Not with all this weighing on her shoulders!

"Until I say so, dammit!" Fischer turned back away from her and peered out the window again. "I won't say it again, Harper. Now get!"

****

Riley left the FBI building in shock and dismay. The fact that she was not suspended meant little to nothing to her at this point. She couldn't care less about the counter facts that Fischer had provided. She did not imagine the phone call, nor did she just make up some random address in the state she'd never been to before. How could Fischer really expect her to give this up? Of course the even bigger question was what could she possibly do to satisfy her request. She had nowhere to go, no one to visit, and nothing came to mind to burn the time.

Once she found a car to rent, and a motel to crash at, Riley found herself falling back into the same routine she usually retreated to when something weighed on her mind. She found the nearest twenty-four-hour gym and checked in for the night. She started with laps in the pool after donning her lap counter watch, her goggles, swim cap, and underwater mp3 player. As much as she tried to focus on the black strip along the floor of the pool, her mind kept replaying everything from that night in Seattle. Perhaps things would have gone differently had she gone to comfort Peter instead of waiting to receive the captain down in the alley.

Riley had a set routine at the gym; a critical order of essential tasks for her to complete. Once her one hundred and fifty laps were done, she dried off and hit the weights. After completing a few sets of bench presses, squats, lunges, curls, and pullups, and still not shaking the sound of Peter's voice, she retreated to the punching bag. She taped up, put on some grappling gloves, and went to town on the bag. She practiced her jabs, crosses, hooks, uppercuts, and overhand punches. Then she graduated to body kicks, low kicks, head kicks, straight teep, side teep, and slapping teep. Then she finished with her knee and elbow strikes; straight, diagonal, step up, and curving knee, uppercut elbow, slashing, and forward elbow thrust.

Each strike that she landed, she saw Peter's face. Every time the bag swung back to meet her, she felt the force of Harold Jensen. Every exhale, she found herself back in the alley, the rain on her neck. Every inhale, she heard that distant scream when she had fallen to her knees in despair. Eventually her hands dropped to her sides, and she rested her head against the bag until it was still. Satisfied with her techniques, and emotionally drained, she unwrapped and headed to the sauna to calm down.

Once showered and cleaned off, she realized that it was well past one a.m. and decided it was time she went home. Driving the empty streets back to her motel, she passed one liquor store after another. She turned up the radio, as if to drown out their calling, but it was no use. By the time she saw the fourth store, she pulled in and got out of the car. Within minutes she had a small shopping cart full of her basic essentials to get over a rough day—Green Spot whiskey, Agavero tequila, pistachios, marshmallows, red licorice, beef jerky, and a box of Reese's Puffs cereal. She ignored the cashier's facial expressions and started back on her trip home.

By the time she got back to her motel she was exhausted; physically, but not mentally. Her body ached for rest, but her mind ran circles and she needed to slow it down before she had any chance of getting sleep. Bunching up the blankets and pillows, she grabbed her snacks and flipped on the television to see what late night programming could get her to sleep the fastest. The first channel was a gameshow; someone had just won a million dollars, and the confetti was filling the screen. Riley grabbed the remoted and clicked it to flip the channel.

Click.

"Did you hear what Stacie wore on the red

carpet last night?" A rerun of one of those all-female talk shows. Riley couldn't roll her eyes hard enough.

Click.

"If you buy right now, we'll give you two more for free!" Another squeegee sales commercial, as if anyone was waiting up at almost two a.m. hoping to find the next best kitchen cleaning item.

Click.

"We've got to get out of here. Beam us up, now!" A space opera serial from back in the day. She used to love these old episodes, but they became kind of corny over time. A couple uniformed starship officers being broken down to the molecular level and teleported back to their ship.

Click.

Wait.

She flipped back.

"I hate teleporters! Disassembling my body and transporting it across time and space! It's terrifying!" Riley stared at the screen, dumbstruck in her revelation. She argued with herself. *It isn't possible. That's just silly. They couldn't have…* But her attempts at convincing herself to drop it had failed.

Within moments her snacks were moved to the side, and her laptop now occupied their space. She began combing through the search engines for real life cases of teleportation. Of course, nothing popped up but conspiracy theory sites and fan forums. She searched as many different key words she could think of, digging through fanfiction, different phrases, minimizing her search parameters, but she came up with nothing. Her eyes were getting heavy, her motivation was dwindling, and before long her will to stay away had dissolved. Her body had finally caught up with her, and it was time to sleep.

****

A knock at the door woke Riley up; persistent and loud. She groaned and opened her eyes to the midday sun glaring through the window. She could have sworn she'd just closed her eyes, but the clock said eleven-thirty a.m. and she could heard the housekeeper asking to come in. Riley groaned again and dismissed the maid as her rubbed her aching head and stared at her face in the mirror, annoyed at the indentions on across her face from the keyboard she had slept on all night.

Sighing, she turned back to her computer and realized the screen was still on. Rubbing her eyes, she brought the computer to the desk and sat down. Apparently she had found something of interest before passing out. She had pulled up an article and highlighted some of the text. The headline read "Son Claims Father Was Murdered" with the subtitle "Claims Included A Female Assassin With Teleportation Abilities." Scanning the bulk of the article, the text described a girl that touched her skin before being engulfed in a bright colorful light and disappearing. Riley suddenly sat up and tried to focus on that night in the alley. Just before the explosion, and the bodies hitting the ground, she had seen a bright green light. *Could this be the same thing?*

Suddenly her browser window closed. Riley stared confused at her computer as she brought her cursor back over the browser icon and opened it again. Almost immediately the window shut again. When she attempted to repeat her previous step, the cursor did not react to her motion. Instead, it slowly scrolled over to her notepad and opened up a new note. As Riley watched, letters began to appear on the notepad, four specific uppercase letters to form a very clear and somber word: **STOP.**

"What the hell is this," Riley muttered as she clicked the power button again and again. When that didn't work, she tried control-alt-delete, but that didn't work either. Then the word began to delete itself until the notepad was once again blank. Riley took a breath, but before she could exhale, her computer turned off. "No, no, no!"

Riley pressed the power button again, but no response. Flipping it over, Riley ejected the battery from the machine, and then put it back in; nothing.

"Dammit!" This wasn't going to stop her. Clearly someone wanted her to stop, but it only confirmed her belief that this was far beyond paranoia. There had been brief moments when she had wondered if, in her drunken state, she had made up the whole thing; maybe she just couldn't accept that Peter was gone. Now she knew, however, that her instincts were right. She grabbed her things and left the room. She knew where she needed to go.

****

When Riley arrived at the Omaha Public Library, she found the bank of public computers and signed into an anonymous server. She knew that whoever had shut down her laptop was either directly watching her, or watching for certain things that she had searched for. Either way, even on an anonymous server, using a computer not registered to her, she knew she was limited on time.

She started with the article about the son who claimed his father was killed by an assassin with teleportation abilities. The boy's name was Eugene Pierce, and his family was one of the richest in America. She had remembered hearing about the trial briefly on the news, but never honed in on the details of the case. Riley was surprised at how little she could actually find on the case. It was almost as if someone had wiped all traces of it, save for brief articles that had little sustenance. All she could find was that Eugene never budged on his testimony, as crazy as it sounded, and eventually the charges were suspiciously dropped despite a mountain of evidence against him. The only article she could find on Eugene involved him checking into a psychiatric facility five years after the trial. Summerhill Asylum, in Maine.

"Guess I know where I'm going then. Hope I'm not the crazy one." Riley printed flight tickets and headed for the door.

****

"Here are you papers for tomorrow's meeting, sir."

"Thank you, Stacey. Have a nice night." Agent Fischer put the papers in his binder and placed it in the briefcase.

Just as he was about to turn off the light and shut his office door, a beep came from his desktop. Fischer groaned and checked his watch. He wanted nothing more than to leave it be until tomorrow, but he had an idea of what it might be, and knew it couldn't wait. Fischer shut his office door and returned to his desk. The alert on his screen confirmed his assumption, and left him no choice. He sighed as he picked up his phone and dialed the number he had been given.

"This is Agent Fischer. SCID: bravo-tango-five-niner-hotel. I need to speak to him." There wasn't an acknowledgment, or a tone at the other end. Fischer waited in silence until he heard a click and then a voice.

"This is Locke." Fischer heard the man sigh as he spoke. "I'm guessing you failed to convince Agent Harper to drop her investigation."

"I'm sorry, sir." Fischer rubbed the bridge of his nose as he looked down at the floor in defeat. "I told her to take some vacation, but it appears she's taking a trip to Summerhill instead. Should I freeze her flight and detain her at the airport?"

There was silence on the other end.

"No. Let her go. We'll take over surveillance from here." The line clicked. Fischer put down the phone and stood in his office, alone in the dark, for a moment.

"Good luck, Harper."

Joshua D. Howell

4 HEAD OVER HEELS

Northern Maine, Near The Canadian Border

Summerhill was a privately owned facility, tucked away in the northern forests of Maine, not too far off from Quebec City. The drive was about four hours from the airport, and Riley had decided to record her notes from those she had taken on the plane. She had used the airport's wifi to print off as much as she could find on the Pierce family and the case against Eugene.

"Case notes, tape one: While it may have stemmed from a drunken night of web searching, I have convinced myself to utilize my paid time off by desperately attempting to connect what happened to Officer Drake with the infamous Pierce Murder from ten years ago.

"The Pierce family, out of Bridgeport, Connecticut, was known mainly for Reynolds Pharmaceuticals. Mrs. Pierce, formerly Jane Reynolds, was the CEO of the international company, until she died in a car crash fifteen years ago.

"She was survived by her husband, Ronald Pierce, and her thirteen-year-old son, Eugene; both of whom were also in the car at the time of the crash. Ronald continued to serve as director of the company's philanthropy division. Five years later, Ronald Pierce was found dead in his home. His throat was cut open and he suffered a deep stab wound through his right temple.

"Eugene Pierce was initially charged with the murder of his father. He claimed to have witnessed an international female student, a guest of the family for the summer, kill his father and then 'teleport' out of the house. The case eventually closed due to lack of evidence, which was highly suspicious given the inexcusable evidence that led to him being charged in the first place.

"Eugene disappeared for five years after that. He had no online presence, no official address, and nothing to tie him down to any specific place. It had been rumored that he had fled the country in fear of a retrial. Then he showed up at Summerhill Asylum and checked himself in voluntarily. He has resided there for the past five years."

Hearing herself speaking her notes aloud didn't help the fact that they sounded like utter dysfunction. In the years that she'd been with the FBI , she would have never made such a leap as to think that there was actually a connection here. Her gut told her that there was something to it, but her brain couldn't help but remind her how much of a stretch this really was. What else was she supposed to do? She had been ordered to go somewhere and do something. As she approached the gate for Summerhill, however, she began to wonder if this was truly a good idea.

The grounds were built like a military base or a prison. A tall, fortified double fence encircled the campus. Once she cleared the front gate, she followed the long drive up a hill towards a visitor's parking lot. The architecture of the main building was absolutely stunning in an 1800s English manor sort of way. She had looked up the facility on the flight over. A massive administration building served as the entrance to the facility. The building then connected to patient living areas via a long singular corridor. There were three patient wings. Two courtyards separated the wings and a corridor connected the wings on the south and north ends. It was a massive facility.

After checking in with reception, Riley waited in the lobby for what felt like hours. She pored over her notes, but she had them memorized at this point. She had been moving at a nonstop pace since Omaha, and the uncomfortable plastic lobby chair wasn't enough to keep her from nodding off. Fifty minutes passed before she was woken by the hideously annoyed voice of the head nurse.

"Agent Harper? Wake up, Agent!"

"I'm up, I'm up." Riley adjusted her eyes to see an elderly woman in a white coat standing over her, tightly gripping a clipboard as if she was considering using it as a motivational tool.

"My name is Beverley Pine. I'm the head nurse here at Summerhill. I apologize for the wait, but I did not know you were coming."

Riley rose to her feet, stretching, and offered her hand to Nurse Pine; it was not received.

"Couldn't be helped, unfortunately, it wasn't necessarily a planned trip." Nurse Pine just stood there, glaring at Riley with one eyebrow raised and the heaviest frown that a human being could possibly muster. "I'm here to visit with a patient of yours. Mr. Eugene Pierce."

"Yes, the receptionist made me aware. You're lucky he's willing to see you, otherwise your trip would have been nothing but a waste of time for us both." Nurse Pine let that linger in the air for a moment before abruptly turning her back and heading for a pair of double doors. "Follow me, Agent."

Riley followed Nurse Pine through the double doors and through another secured door that led to the main corridor leading to the patient wings. Along the side of the corridor stood a woman in a patient gown with long stringy gray hair, holding a mop while she stared down Riley. Nurse Pine made a noise that could only be described as a quick *hiss* and the patient quickly lowered her head and returned to work.

"I don't believe Mr. Pierce has ever granted a visit in his five-year stay with us." Nurse Pine spoke with a groan in her voice, keeping her face forward, more to fill the silence than to actually engage Riley.

"He's had other callers then, since checking himself in?"

"Oh, yes. We don't get many celebrities up here. The press, or what qualifies for press these days, used to come for weeks, trying to get an exclusive sit down with him. He never accepted once." The two reached the end of the corridor, stepped through another secured door and headed towards wing two.

Riley started to see more patients and attendants walking about.

"Interesting. How has Eugene kept himself in the past five years? Any misconduct during his stay?"

"Oh, no, not at all. We separated him at first, but now he is free to the common areas like most everyone else. We do house some criminals here, but they are locked in the far wing."

"Criminals? Really? I thought asylums for the criminally insane didn't really exist anymore."

"For the most part they don't. Most people deemed criminally insane are sent to hospital wards of larger government prisons. There is a market, however, for private companies to relieve some of the prisons by taking in those with lessor crimes, so long as the private facilities match the minimum security requirements. Criminal patients make up one third of our patient population here at Summerhill."

"Impressive." Walking down the main hallway for wing two, the pair came to a large room that appeared to be in the middle of the wing. The room had glass windows and sliding doors on either side that opened to each of the enclosed courtyards. There were couches, bookshelves, a few television sets, and card tables scattered about the room. The patients that were in the room didn't seem to even notice Riley's presence, but did seem to make an effort to avoid making eye contact with Nurse Pine.

"This is one of our common rooms, recently refurbished a few years back. We have one of these in the middle of each wing, with the exception of the criminal wing. We like to encourage relaxation for our patients during their stay. When they aren't in treatment or counseling sessions, patients can spend that majority of their day in here until the nine p.m. curfew."

"That makes sense." Riley didn't really know what else to say. At this point she was only speaking to fill the gaps in Nurse Pine's speech. She peered around the room as they walked through. The natural sunlight was a nice touch to the otherwise plain looking room. The floors, walls, and ceilings were painted with an off white color, save for a large black circle on the floor in the middle of the room. For a moment she thought to ask, but decided not to extend her tour any longer than it needed to be.

"We don't have many meeting rooms that patients are allowed to use. This interrogation room will have to do. We use this for when an attorney wishes to visit their criminal client. Mr. Pierce is restrained for your safety, though I doubt you will have any issues."

Riley gave a half smile as she walked past Nurse Pine through the opened door.

****

As the door shut behind her, Riley looked across the room to see a young man in his late twenties in a blue shirt, with blue eyes and short slick brown hair. Eugene Pierce sat in his chair, his hands on the table with steel cuffs around each wrist connected to the table via chain. He looked up to meet her gaze and smiled. Riley broke his stare as she placed her papers on the table and took her seat.

"Good afternoon, Mr. Pierce. I'm Agent Harper with the FBI. I appreciate you granting my visit."

"Agent? Well, what an honor." Eugene had a sarcastic tone in his voice as he smiled back at Riley. He raised his hands a bit from the table, pulling the chain tight. "I'd shake your hand, but I don't have much of a reach right now."

"I'm working a case at the moment that I was wondering if you might be able to help me with." Eugene stared back at Riley with an intrigued look upon his face.

"Now, just how could I be of help to an FBI Agent?"

"The case is mostly unrelated but has some similarities with the death of your father. I apologize for bringing up the past, but I was hoping you would be willing to tell me your story to see if my hunch is correct." Riley tried to keep a straight face as she stared back at Eugene. She did not want to come off as desperate, but she didn't want to leave empty handed.

"My story, huh?" Eugene chuckled and massaged his chin in his hand. "Well, I guess it's been awhile since I told it. And how often do I really ever get the chance. Not too many conversationalists in here."

"Do you mind if I record it, Mr. Pierce?" Riley held up a small mp3 recorder in her hand. Eugene frowned for a second, and then returned to his charming painted-on smile.

"I would rather you not. But you may take hand-written notes if you wish."

Riley was confused as to the difference between the two, but nodded and put away the recorder. She grabbed her notepad and clicked her pen.

"Okay, then. Ready when you are." Riley put her pen to paper and stared back at Eugene. He smirked, and then leaned back in his chair, as much as one could with their hands cuffed to the table.

****

The Pierce Manor - Bridgeport, Connecticut
10 Years Ago

When Eugene was young, he longed for the stars, to see them, to be among them, to know them more than simply lights in the night. He never wanted to be an astronaut, because even in adolescence he knew that astronauts had to return. Eugene didn't want to return, he wanted to leave. There were planets he had never heard of, there were sights he had never seen, there were suns he had never felt a warmth from. More than his passion, more than an escape, this was a trap. For this persistent yearning, for something he knew would never come to pass, would always remain with him. A night wouldn't pass when he didn't drift off into the cosmos, as if returning home, and find a clarity in the cold vacuum of space. Nothing haunted him more, until he met her.

On the eve of summer, after his graduation from boarding school, Eugene had returned home to the Pierce Academy for Gifted Youth. Though the establishment had only existed since the 1980s, the Academy had enough standing to lure some of the great young minds at the end of the twentieth century. Eugene never attended it, as his father felt it was a conflict of interest. In the summers, when he wasn't living in the barracks at the boarding school, Eugene lived in the east wing of the Academy with his father, the Dean of the Academy. The great Ronald Pierce, philanthropist and scholar, ran the Academy as part of an outreach program partnered with Reynolds Pharmaceuticals; Eugene's late mother's company.

The purpose of the Academy was to host gifted students from around the world for a semester or two throughout the year. While enrolled, they would attend legendary lectures from some of the top heads of all fields of business. Ronald Pierce was not heavily involved during the school year, but he would host a single student over the summer. One lucky student, the top of the class, would have the honor of staying with Mr. Pierce's family for the summer interim. Whatever specialty they were interested in, Mr. Pierce would fund a three month internship with a company that reigned supreme in that field. The student would then spend their nights with Mr. Pierce's family and reflect with Mr. Pierce as to what they'd learned. It was a coveted honor.

Having spent the last two summers away from home on school trips, Eugene realized that this was, in fact, the first time he had been home in three years. The doors still creaked as if they hadn't been moved in ages. The front hall remained as vast and empty as ever. The quiet was overwhelmingly peaceful. School was out, and for a moment, Eugene was certain that he was perfectly alone, and felt a deep satisfaction. As he strolled down the east corridor, Eugene passed paintings, photographs, and busts of some of the most majestic individuals in history. The Academy may not have been around for very long, but it held respect for the past within its thick walls and solemn hallways.

When Eugene arrived at the end of the long corridor his heart caved in. He had longed so much to return home, and now he felt as if he had never left. Although it was originally designed to sit apart from the Academy, Ronald wanted the Pierce Manor connected, so that he could always be attached to his work in some form or another. The dueling marble staircases rose up to the resident chambers, the dining hall, and other family rooms. The main floor led to the Dean's office and study, the library, and a lavish ballroom. His father was out for the weekend, but it wasn't a surprise to Eugene. No staff could be seen or heard, and so it felt as if he would have the manor to himself, to relax and enjoy.

Once the staircase was conquered, Eugene made his way down the hall to the living quarters, past his mother's former painting room, past the television room, to the door at the end of the hall; his room. When he was younger, he had always dreaded his return home; fearing that his father had cleared out his room, and that there would be nothing be a blank space on the other side of the door. He had always opened the door to find his room had remained untouched, but it didn't stop him from having the same fear the following year. Now, with three years gone by since he had last come home, he returned to that same fear.

Grabbing the handle, he twisted it and pushed the old door open. The idea of closing his eyes had crossed his mind, but he braved his way through the door and stepped into the room. There wasn't a blank space, but his room was not there either. Instead the walls have been painted, some of the furniture had been moved, and the bed had been replaced with something more elegant. *What is this?* He immediately went to the walk-in closet. Opening it, he found that his stash of childhood memories had been removed. Now there were someone else's clothes and items hanging on display.

He turned around, planning on finding the closest staff member and demanding an explanation, only to come screeching to a halt when he saw the most gorgeous girl he had ever seen. She was walking out of his bathroom, without a shred of clothing save for the towel she was using to wrap her wet hair in. She couldn't have been more than five-and-a-half feet, with the tiniest of frames. She clearly had some athletic background, as the majority of her was toned to some degree. Her skin was flawless, with the exception of one tattoo on her right forearm—an anchor.

It wasn't the first time Eugene had seen a naked girl, but he couldn't help but stay frozen in place, unsure of what to do. Obviously there had been some kind of mistake, and no matter what he did, it was going to be an awkward exchange. For a second he pondered the idea of simply remaining in his frozen state and waiting for her to obliviously re-enter the bathroom so that he could make his escape unseen. That, however, was not going to happen. Before he could think of an alternative, the girl suddenly looked up and immediately screamed at him. Not in fear, but in anger.

"Hey! What the hell are you doing in here?"

He was about to apologize and beg forgiveness for his intrusion, but then Eugene remembered that this was in fact his room to begin with.

"What am I doing here? What are you doing here? This is my room, lady!"

The girl didn't even stop to cover herself as she leapt over the bed and attacked him. Before he knew it, Eugene was pinned against the wall, unable to do anything but stare in shock at the scrawny little girl who'd managed to get the drop on him and render him completely helpless.

"I will not be subjected to your perverted ambitions." She spoke with such a commanding presence, backed by clear rage within her eyes. He considered fighting back, but felt it would only escalate the situation. Fortunately, before anything else had a chance to happen, one of his father's maids came rushing into the room to break them apart. The maid handed the girl a second towel, and quickly grabbed Eugene's arm and escorted him out of the room.

"I am so sorry, Mr. Pierce. I did not hear you arrive. I was under the impression you wouldn't be back for another day or so. I would have informed you that your bedroom had been moved."

"Moved? For what reason?" Eugene was beyond irritated at this point, having his peaceful homecoming so abruptly interrupted. As the maid continued to pull him down the hallway, Eugene looked back to see the girl slamming the door shut. "And who the hell is she?"

"Your father felt that your room was best suited for guests, and so he had your things moved to your mother's old painting room."

Eugene's irritation continued to increase. "The rooms are practically the same, Sharon. I can't think of any logical reason for my father to move my things other than to piss me off when I returned."

"Oh, no, Mr. Pierce. That is not the case at all. Your mother's old painting room has been refurbished and it is better suited for your return home." The maid opened the door and motioned for

Eugene to enter. Eugene saw his bed sitting in the middle of the bare room. "Let us know what other furniture items you require and we will have them brought up in the morning."

"You didn't answer my question, Sharon." Eugene sighed and threw his bag onto the bed as he wandered over to the window. "Who is the girl in my room?"

"That would be Ms. Juliet Cubro." The maid passed Eugene to open the curtains and let the light fill the room. "She is your father's ward for the summer for winning top honors this year at the Academy."

"Great, just great. So she's going to be here the whole summer? After what just happened?"

The maid smiled and patted Eugene on the shoulder. "I'm sure you'll manage." As the maid left Eugene to stare at the blank walls of his new room, she stopped only to say one more thing before closing his door. "Welcome home, Mr. Pierce."

****

The first couple weeks were rough. Everyone met for breakfast and dinner at the main dining table. Eugene's father was his normal distant self, and Juliet obviously had not gotten over the incident. This left Eugene to be the silent party at all group occasions no matter what he tried to do to change it. Finally he broke and caught Juliet in the hallway.

"Hey, uh, I wanted to say I'm sorry. You know, for walking in on you like that." Juliet stared at him, as if she was waiting for something more. "Look, you're going to be here for the whole summer, and things don't need to be this awkward. Could we move past this?"

"Ice cream."

"Ice cream," Eugene repeated, hoping to spark more words.

"Yes. Tomorrow. You can pick me up from the institute and buy me ice cream." With that, she left him, standing in the hallway, speechless.

****

In due time, things changed for Eugene. Suddenly he wanted to know everything about the new house guest. Juliet came from Bosnia, or rather, Bosnia and Herzegovin, as Juliet always corrected him. During the day, she interned at the Helman Science Institute where she studied advanced physics in line with several major studies being conducted on a global scale. Eugene couldn't make heads or tails of her work, but he was willing to listen. After the first day of ice cream, there was another, and another, until he no longer picked her up in his car, but walked her home instead. They would take different routes, through the park, or down a residential row; anything to prolong their time together.

It was destined to happen. It wasn't like they could avoid each other, even in a place as large as the Pierce Manor. Each evening, Juliet would play a game of chess with Mr. Pierce and discuss what she learned that day. Afterwards, she would meet up with Eugene for a late night flick, or lounging on the roof watching stars. While Juliet didn't necessarily talk much about her life, Eugene could sense a troubled past. She never mentioned her family, or what life was like back at home. Juliet, on the other hand, constantly asked about Eugene's past. He eventually opened up to her more than any of the several counselors he was forced to endure after the death of his mother. Juliet presented easier company, and he couldn't help but find himself lost in her presence; stress-free and elegant. He was falling for her, head over heels, and there was nothing he could do about it.

The night finally came when the two had talked long past the midnight hour and had absolutely no intention of leaving the other's side. Her lips met his, and Eugene felt as if he had left a ledge with no possibility of saving himself. He returned her kiss and brought her closer to him, and that sealed both their fates. Before long the two were entangled, arms and legs wrapped around each other, as their hands and lips explored the other. It never went much further than that, as the two feared that the maid, or someone worse, would suddenly appear the absolute moment a single piece of clothing was removed. So the two kissed until they passed out in each other's arms. It was the first peaceful moment that Eugene had truly felt in ages. That peace, to Eugene's dismay, was not to last.

The following evening, after returning from a late bike ride around the city, Eugene came home to find Juliet and his father engrossed in another intense chess match. Eugene crept past the doorway to the reading room, not wanting to disturb them, but stopped short of heading upstairs when he heard raised voices. This was clearly not a conversation about physics, but Eugene couldn't make out what they were saying. Creeping back to the doorway, Eugene peered in to see Juliet knock over the chessboard in rage.

"I can explain, Juliet. You don't understand." Eugene's father sounded distressed as he struggled to speak. Eugene had never known his father to not conduct his conversations in a confident, steadfast manner.

"Don't! You know why I'm here. You deserve this!" Juliet stood up from her game chair and stared down Mr. Pierce. Before Eugene could chime in with a half-witted attempt at humor, Juliet brandished a long tactical knife from her side.

Wait. Eugene tried to speak, but it was too late. In fact, he couldn't tell if he had managed to actually make a sound in protest before Juliet lunged over the game table. The blade slid across Ronald Pierce's neck like butter, and his eyes pleaded for mercy as his collar was soaked within seconds. Before Ronald could even raise his hands to cover the wound, Juliet shoved the entire length of the blade deep into Ronald's right temple; one hand on the handle, the other palm pressing against the butt of the knife to deliver one swift blow.

Ronald made a sucking noise as he struggled to breath, but it eventually died as Juliet pulled the knife out. He blinked a few times, as his vision began to blur, and only then realized that Eugene was watching from the doorway. He tried to smile in Eugene's direction, but lost the ability to move halfway through the attempt. As Mr. Pierce's body slouched over on the sofa, staining its cream-colored cushions with spurts of crimson, Eugene finally found the strength to speak.

"What…what did you do?" He tried, but he couldn't make sense of what he just saw. The gorgeous girl who he had spent the last two most courting, now stood over his dead father, catching her breath as if she had just scored the winning point in some kind of sporting match. At the sound of Eugene's voice, Juliet jumped and turned around in shock. "What the hell did you just do?"

"Eugene!" Juliet dropped the knife to the floor and raised her hands in front of her. "Please. You don't understand."

"Understand what?" Eugene was shouting now, as the adrenaline kicked in. "You just killed my dad! What the hell else is there to understand?"

"Eugene, I'm so sorry!" Juliet began to walk toward him. "This wasn't about you. I'm so sorry you had to see that."

"Don't come any closer." Eugene backed away until he bumped into the barrel of umbrellas. He looked down and grabbed his father's old wooden softball bat and brought it to his side. His hand tightened around the grip as he stared, conflicted, back at Juliet.

"Don't do this Eugene. I've never wanted to hurt you," Juliet pleaded with so much sincerity in her voice that for a brief second, Eugene's grip loosened around the bat. Then Eugene saw his father's body twitching on the sofa.

"I'm sorry." Eugene leaped forward and swung the bat down upon Juliet. Juliet crossed her

Joshua D. Howell

arms in front of her as the bat came crashing down. The bulk of the bat splintered in a hundred pieces upon contact with Juliet's skin. Eugene stepped back stood there with the broken bat in his hand. He looked back and forth from the bat to Juliet. There wasn't a scratch on her, and the room was covered with wood chips.

"Please Eugene," Juliet said, as she once again stretched out her arms to plead with him. "Let's talk about this."

Eugene didn't have time to process what just happened, but instead dropped the bat and tackled Juliet to the floor. He could feel the flames from the fireplace light his face, as Eugene kneeled over Juliet and slammed his fist down upon her. Juliet blocked the blow and kicked Eugene off her. As she stood, Eugene threw the chess board at her. Juliet swiped the board away only to be met with a fist across her face. Before she could regain her focus, Eugene had grabbed her by the shoulders and hurled her into the glass bookcase.

****

As she fell to the floor amongst the glass and fallen papers, she considered staying there. She had no will to fight Eugene, but as he stood over her with rage in his veins, she knew she had no choice. Juliet rose to her feet and stretched her leg to kick Eugene in the face. She shoved her shoulder into his chest, and then spun her elbow around to catch him in the chin. Wrapping her leg around to trip him, Juliet shoved Eugene back, sending him head over heels into game table.

****

Arching his back in pain on the floor, Eugene looked up to see the lifeless body of his father lying above him on the sofa. Focusing his eyes, Eugene saw the knife lying on the floor beside him. As he reached for it in fury, he could hear Juliet begging for him to stop.

"I'm sorry, Eugene. I'm so sorry." As Eugene grabbed the knife and turned back around to meet her, Juliet touched the anchor tattoo on her forearm. "I'm leaving now."

Eugene threw the knife towards her as the room became engulfed in bright light. Suddenly, Juliet was gone, and the knife passed through the space where she had been and dug itself into the family photo hanging on the wall behind where she had stood.

****

Summerhill, Present

"I sat there, staring at the knife, deep in the wall through the last family picture we had all taken together, when both my parents were still alive and happy. I struggled to get off the floor and ended up sitting on the couch beside my father's body. I didn't move until the police arrived. I didn't even hear them bust down the door. I was so lost in it all, trying to piece together what all had just happened. I had no idea how screwed I really was.

"Of course no one believed my story. To my surprise, there were no records of Juliet's stay at the manor. The maid could not be located, and no witnesses could be found to corroborate my story. The prosecutor had his case wrapped up like a fruit basket. They had my fingerprints on the knife, and my only defense was a science fiction story about a female assassin who teleported away from the crime scene. And yet, at the end of the trial, I wasn't convicted. My jaw nearly hit the desk when they said I was being released for lack of evidence.

"It was clear to me then that someone had paid someone else off, and that I was merely a pawn in some grander scheme. Perhaps it was a last favor from my parents' company. Whoever it was, they never contacted me, and I never went looking." Eugene sighed as he massaged his hands and stared down at the table. There was a moment of silence before he regained composure and looked back up at Riley with his charming smile once again. "Anyway, that's my story. It's a crazy one, huh?"

"Well, that's one word for it." Riley looked back at Eugene. Usually she could tell the difference between someone giving her a story and someone telling her the truth, but this guy had her stumped. The story was so farfetched it was beyond belief, but Riley couldn't help but believe it when he said it. "Where did you go for the following five years before admitting yourself to Summerhill?"

"I just...went away." Eugene leaned back again, finding his comfort zone again after obviously hitting an uncomfortable spot. "Tabloids can be harsh, and all the money in the world couldn't get the paparazzi off my back. I went here and there, until I just got tired of hiding. It began as a joke, but the more I thought about that night in the manor, the less sure I was of my own sanity. I figured no one would bother me here, so I checked myself in."

The two of them stared at each other for a moment. Riley found this all to be incredibly intriguing but still thought it was a stretch that any of it could truly be related to her case. Suddenly she felt as if she had made this trip for nothing, and wanted nothing more than to get back to Omaha and pick up the search for Peter.

"Well, that's all I needed Mr. Pierce." She stacked her papers back in order and put them back in her folder. Unclicking her pen, she stood and made her way to the door. "Thank you for your time."

"Well I guess I appreciate the visit. Nothing like a twenty-minute conversation to put me back in the crosshairs."

"Excuse me?" Riley stopped at the open door, motioning for the orderly to wait. "Crosshairs? What do you mean?"

"Well, I haven't told that story to anyone in the ten years since the trial." Eugene smirked and bent down to run his fingers through his hair. "If it wasn't a favor from the company, I imagine whoever it was that saved me from prison figured I'd keep my mouth shut. Now I'm here, talking to the FBI. I'm sure that doesn't look good. Probably rubs someone the wrong way."

"You're probably right." Riley almost offered an apologetic smile in Eugene's direction, but instead simply nodded her head and left the room.

If there was any truth to his story, then his logic was sound. She, however, didn't have time to think about it anymore, and instead proceeded to make her way to the closest exit. She needed to get back to more important matters.

Joshua D. Howell

5 RASPBERRIES AND CREAM

Los Angeles

Gasp!

Juliet Cubro woke up in a fright, desperately gasping for air, as if she had been holding her breath through the entire nightmare. She sat up in the dark and held her face in her hands. Her reoccurring nightmares never ceased to bring the worst out of her. They weren't nightly, but they were consistent. She had enough memories to haunt three lifetimes. As her eyes adjusted to the dark, she realized she was still in the penthouse.

"Great. I'm still here." She sighed as she looked back down at the California King she had been sleeping in. There were several people still passed out in the bed. She didn't know who they were, and honestly couldn't remember where she'd met them; likely a club somewhere, or walking the street. Juliet had her own form of special protection from certain ailments that the normal person would be worried about when sleeping with strangers, let alone several of them. She didn't normally wake up in a bed full of guys and gals, so she must have been especially drunk last night.

She climbed out of the bed and made her way across the room. The floor felt cool against her bare feet. She stretched her arms out wide as she yawned. She first hit up the kitchen and grabbed a cold bottle of scotch from the fridge. She liked her scotch cold, no matter how many people frowned when they saw more bottles of liquor than milk in her fridge. Setting the bottle on a table, she made her way to the windows. Grabbing the thick twelve-foot-long curtains, she pulled them open to reveal the L.A. skyline in the bright late afternoon sun. She heard the groans behind her, and immediately was done with the idea of company.

"You have five minutes to leave. I don't want your number, I don't have any handouts, and there is nothing you can take that will get past security downstairs. Do not be here when I get out of the shower, or you will regret we ever met."

Juliet grabbed the bottle and walked past the group as they got dressed. Stepping into the master bathroom, she took a moment to stare at herself in the mirror. She didn't have time for self-pity. She shimmied out of her lacey garments and stepped into the shower, bringing the bottle with her. As she stood under the boiling hot water, taking a swig every now and again, Juliet tried desperately to clear her head. She had a task to do tonight, and she didn't need her nightmares fogging up her concentration. When she realized she was more likely to fall back asleep in the warm shower than anything else, she turned the dial on cold and turned to meet it head on. Once she was good and awake, she left the shower, dried off, and grabbed a knife from the drawer beneath the sink.

Walking back through the suite in her robe, Juliet found that her guests had sufficiently left the premises. Putting the knife away, Juliet walked down the hall and opened a door to her special room. The walls were lined with shelves of mannequin heads sporting different high class wigs, styles and colors galore. She sat down in her favorite chair, in front of a large round makeup mirror and a desk full of supplies. She began to coat her skin with all the essentials to fit the part she intended to play that night. The final touches, a slightly overbearing blush, heavy on the colored eye liner, and a thick coat of ruby red

87

lipstick, completed her objective.

Once she had picked the perfect set of lingerie, she slid her legs into a pair of burgundy nylons with black lace at the top. She pored over her collection of heels until she found just the right pair. Finally, she walked into her closet to pick a dress. She needed something skimpy, but not too trashy. She found the perfect, skin-tight, dark red dress that rode up a little high on her thighs and had a deep slit down the center. Donning her dress and heels, and finishing the look with a flashy necklace, Juliet stood in the mirror and admired her work.

"Ugh. I look like a tramp." Juliet smirked at herself. "This'll work."

****

Raspberries and Cream was a popular nightclub in the ritzy district of downtown Los Angeles. There wasn't a night where three of the four VIP suites weren't occupied by one celebrity or another. Every single night, there was a line out the door and down the block. The skanks, the players, the addicts, they lined up and hoped for the chance to enter. Juliet wasn't someone that stood in a line and waited. She paid the black cab to drive up to the front of the line. When she stepped out of the car she made eye contact with the bouncer, and didn't break it. Ten steps from the curb and she was within inches of the tall, burly man, who at the moment was staring at her with the most impressed expression he could produce.

"You trying to get in, little lady?" Juliet looked up at him, raised her eyebrows and smiled. "Ha-ha. You got style, I'll give you that, but you just side-stepped a hundred-person line."

"I didn't see line." Juliet reached into her purse and produced a hundred dollar bill. Bringing it her lips, she kissed the bill, and then reached forward to tuck the bill inside the left breast pocket of the bouncer's jacket. He laughed again and nodded.

"All right, shawty, you win." The bouncer opened the door and held it for Juliet as she stepped across the threshold into the land full of lights and liquor.

Throwing her purse over her shoulder, Juliet waded into the pool of sweat and testosterone. The DJ had just dropped the new track, some pop song with a new bass beat filter laid on top of it, and suddenly the room was in sync, bumping, grinding, jumping. She surveyed the room until she saw the roped off lounge section. In the middle, surrounded by his posse, was a tall, handsome, Greek god of a man, sipping his champagne and watching the crowd. This was her man.

Juliet let loose, allowing her hips to match the

bass, putting her hands in the air, and adding a slight curve to her stance; perfectly punctuating the right assets. The spotlights played on the crowd and Juliet made sure to stand in a pillar of glorious bring pink. A few songs later, with the right moves in play, Juliet noticed the man's eyes begin to focus on her. She saw him lean over to his buddy on the left, likely asking who she was. When the friend shook his head, Juliet's mark returned his eyes to her. She met his eyes for a second, bit her lip and smiled, and then turned around to let him see the rest of her. When the song ended, she turned around only to find that the roped off section was now completely empty. Before she could think, a hand tapped her on the shoulder, and she turned to see a medium build man in Ray-Bans.

"Mr. Kirsch would like the pleasure of your company in the VIP upstairs. Would you follow me, Miss…?"

"Oh! Miss Summers." She smiled back at the man, gave a ditzy shoulder shrug and nodded. "I'd love to!"

The man led her through the heart of the crowd, making a path for her to follow. Off to the side of the dancefloor was a door with a neon star hanging over head. Once the door shut behind them, the deafening volume of the club was suddenly muted and replaced with quiet jazz pumping through small overhead speakers. The man led Juliet up a curved, carpeted stairway which wrapped its way up two floors until it opened into a large white room complete with leather couches, a personal bar, and a strip of two-way glass that overlooked the entire club. The couches were occupied by three men, multiple women surrounding each of them, with random pieces of clothing strewed out on the floor. At the bar was her man, sipping on a cocktail and smiling back at her. He told the man in the glasses to wait outside and guard the door. Then he turned his attention back to Juliet.

"Don't mind my pals. They're busy and couldn't give a shit about what we do." Kirsch reached out and brushed the side of Juliet's face before grabbing the back of her neck and pulling her into him. "I don't want to know your name. I just want to know your taste."

"Is that so, Mr. Big Shot?" Juliet smiled as Kirsch backed her up into the wall, leaned his arm against the wall above her head and looked down upon her.

"You have a problem with that?" He smiled when she said it, but she knew his aggressive forwardness was far from an act. She grabbed him by his tie and pulled him closer.

"Not at all, baby."

His lips met her neck as his hands roamed over her chest and thighs. As he grabbed one of her legs and lifted it up against him, they locked lips in a deep kiss. They kissed deeply for a moment before Kirsch suddenly retracted his face in pain.

"Ah! What the hell was that?" Kirsch brought a handkerchief to his mouth and noticed that his tongue was bleeding. "Did you just bite me? What do you have, fangs for teeth?"

"Ah, no, baby. I just like it rough." She pulled him back in and began to suck on his neck. He began to relax again. He grabbed her by the back of her head, a fistful of her hair, and yanked her head up to meet his.

"Not too rough, slut."

Juliet smiled with her lips closed. As Kirsch went back to kissing her neck, Juliet let her tongue slide to the roof of her mouth as she pulled back a piece of scar tissue to reveal something metal hiding underneath. She slide the razor blade out from the roof of her mouth and positioned it between her teeth. Smiling, she pulled back from Kirsch and tilted her head.

"Too bad, baby. I like it really rough." In one quick, swift, swipe of her head, Juliet slit Kirsch's throat with the razor blade. Of course the blade made a bloody mess, but it didn't cut deep enough for a fatal blow. Juliet unhooked on of the handles of her purse to reveal a curved blade that she ran across Kirsch's throat for a deeper, definitive cut. As his blood projected over the wall around them, as well as coating the Juliet's neckline and chest, Juliet kneed him in the stomach and kicked him backwards to fall flat on the floor.

"Are you crazy?" The first of the three men to notice their leader bleeding out on the carpet jumped up, shoving his women off him.

"Holy shit!" The second man looked like he was about to hurl as the women began to scream and bunch together in the corner of the room.

"You are so dead, bitch!" The third man, a stocky fellow with a scar across his cheek, stood up and pointed at Juliet as he spoke. Juliet unhooked the other handle from her purse to produce another blade. Folding the purse inside out, Juliet unhooked a final clasp as the metal lining of the purse gave way to become a thin, long chain connecting the two daggers in her hands.

"Yea? Well come get this bitch."

The three man began to smile as they removed their suit jackets and stood next to each other, cracking their knuckles and chuckling.

"You're going to pay for that," said the one with the scar. "Slowly and painfully."

"Oh, stop teasing me." Juliet shed her heels and began to bounce on her feet as the music changed from a jazz ballad an upbeat rock melody. Letting one blade fall out of her hand towards the floor, giving the chain some slack, Juliet smiled as she began to spin the blade and chain around her. Spinning the blade a few times over her head like a cowgirl with a whip, Juliet brought it down and crisscrossed it back and forth in front of her. The men slowly began to lose their confidence as they tried to follow the dagger with their eyes. Juliet jumped off the carpet, spinning sideways in the air, pulling the chain up and over her, until she landed back on both feet and sent the blade flying forward to dig itself deep into the chest of scar face.

Juliet yanked back on the chain, pulling free the blade, and opening up a gaping hole in the man's chest that quickly began to spray its red fluid across the room. The other two men just stood there as they watched their friend fall to his knees and hit the floor.

"Wow, you guys suck." The two turned back to Juliet, swapping their fear for anger. "Am I really going to have to do all the work?"

"I've got her," the one on the left said as he reached in side his jacket for his gun. Juliet sent a flying dagger straight into his elbow and pulled it back, forcing the man to scream out in pain as his arm was extended. Having already grabbed his gun, he pulled back on the trigger in pain and sprayed the room with bullets. As the bullets dug holes into the wall, up through the popcorn ceiling, and even hitting a couple of the women in the corner, Juliet pulled tight, extended her leg, and stepped down on the chain, forcing the man's gun to point down and shoot himself in the foot.

Juliet twisted around to thrust the other dagger into the belly of the third man who had lunged towards her in the desperate hope of tackling her to ground. Yanking the dagger out of guy's belly, Juliet wrapped the chain around his neck, pulled tight, and then dropped to the floor to slide her way through his legs. Pulling all the way through, Juliet sent the man face first into the floor as he desperately tried to loosen the chain. Juliet let go and walked over the second man, still screaming in pain from the gunshot to his own foot. The man attempted to raise the gun towards her, but Juliet quickly snatched it from his hand, flipped it around, and shot the man in the face. Turning around, Juliet aimed the gun at the third man just getting to his feet and pulled the trigger three more times until the man hit the floor again.

While the constant booming of the club's bass had drowned out the gunfire before any of the crowd on the dancefloor could hear it, Kirsch's men at the bottom of the stairs must have. As the first one made it to the top of the stairs, Juliet threw the empty gun at his face. In the following seconds, Juliet pulled the dagger out of the dead man's elbow, ran up the side of the wall, leaped, and shoved the blade deep into the man's skull. Flipping over his falling body, Juliet sprung herself off his back to fly down the stairs and tackle the remaining guard, Mr. Ray-Bans, mid-air. As Juliet repeatedly jabbed the man's throat with her blade, she rode him like a flying carpet down the stairs until the two hit the bottom.

Juliet pushed herself off him, and laid there on the floor for a moment. Taking a breath, Juliet attempted to wipe the excessive blood splatter from her face. Eventually she ceased the useless act, and brought herself to her feet. Stepping through the VIP door, Juliet made her way across the dancefloor just as the strobe lights kicked in. The beat hit hard and the crowd began to jump. Breathing in deep and smiling, Juliet couldn't help but jump as well as the crowd around her danced oblivious to her blood-soaked skin and attire. Juliet made her way to the other side of the dancefloor and pushed through the exit door into the dark alley. As soon as the door shut behind her, she ran.

The adrenaline pushed her to achieve the ultimate stride as she barreled down the alley, crossed the street and continued down the next for a few blocks before stopping outside of a the staff entrance for a Chinese restaurant. She grabbed a hose attached to the building and turned it on. She sprayed herself down and kept in the shadows and waited. Within moments she heard the screams as people escaped the club into the alley blocks away. Dropping the hose, Juliet grabbed an orange bag from the dumpster, opened it and pulled out her getaway clothes. Ditching the dress and donning pair of jeans and a hoodie, Juliet grabbed her phone and continued jogging down the alley.

Reaching the street, Juliet pulled off her blonde wig and threw it in a trashcan. Pulling the hoodie over her short, buzzed cut hair, Juliet jogged towards a bus making its stop and hopped on. After paying the fare, Juliet plopped down in a seat towards the back, scrunched down against the window, and got out her phone. Opening up a secure e-mail application, Juliet typed a message to the party who hired her.

The job is done; target eliminated.

Putting the phone down, Juliet peered out the window as the bus turned down the street and drove a few blocks till it passed the club. Police cars were just starting to show up as the people stupid enough to stick around were corralled to the side of the building for pat downs and holding.

Her phone dinged, and Juliet frowned as she

picked it up. The party that hired her shouldn't have been able to e-mail her back, considering she used a dark net masked source to send her confirmation in the first place. After scanning her immediate surroundings, to make sure she was in a safe place to check her phone, Juliet grabbed it from her purse. Turning on the screen, Juliet suddenly sat up straight in shock as she read the message flashing in red on her phone.

Alert! Alarm Trip: Summerhill.

"Eugene!"

6 DATE AT THE DINER

Northern Maine, Near The Canadian Border

When Riley left Summerhill, feeling like she'd wasted the past twenty-four hours pursing the most half-assed lead she had ever entertained, she immediately looked up flight options once she strapped herself into her rental. To her dismay, the next flight wasn't until late the next day. When that fact set in, and she realized she would need to spend the night in Maine, Riley suddenly became aware of just how tired she was.

About a mile or two down the road from Summerhill was a hotel and diner. As much as she wanted to get further away from her disappointing afternoon, Riley knew she wouldn't make it another minute behind the wheel. After securing a room and dropping off her things, Riley walked across the gravel parking lot, under the starlit sky, to the open-late diner across the road. Upon entering, Riley noticed only one other patron, an old man drinking coffee in a corner booth. Riley took one of the bar stools and gave the menu a quick look over as the waitress came over.

"Evening, sweetie. What can I get ya?" The older woman waited patiently with her pen and notepad in hand as Riley scanned the menu.

"Let me get the club sandwich on wheat, light on the mayo, and a glass of whatever you have on tap."

The waitress nodded and put the slip on the rotating wheel for the cook to grab.

"Here you go, sweetie. Let me know if you need anything else." The waitress set down a pint glass of wheat beer on a coaster in front of Riley and went into the back. Before Riley could even get a sip in, a tall black man in jeans and a long-sleeve thermal shirt sat down on the barstool directly next to her.

"Hi, there. I'm Steve." The man was muscular, his head was bald, his hands appeared smooth, and his crisp smile matched his deep seductive voice. Riley chose not to look at him, but instead stared at his reflection in one of the glass-framed pictures along the bar. "Having a late night meal, huh? Can't sleep?"

"Hi, Steve." Riley continued to drink her beer and ignore making any physical recognition of his presence. The man was certainly handsome, and kind of her type, but she was far from in the mood. "All these empty chairs and you picked that one, huh?"

"Yeah, well, I guess I like company when I eat." The man chuckled and scanned over the menu. "Don't you like company?"

Riley took another gulp of her beer until the waitress came around and dropped off her plate. Riley motioned for a refill as she downed the last of the pint and continued to ignore the man sitting next to her. The waitress brought over the second pint and asked if the gentleman wanted anything. He waved her off, and turned back to Riley.

"Are you here to visit Summerhill? That's really the only reason outsiders come around here."

"Well, aren't you the detective." Riley took a bite out of her sandwich and sent a smile towards the waitress at the end of the bar. The waitress returned the smile and once again went into the back. Out of the corner of her eye, Riley saw the man writing something down on a napkin. "If you're writing down your number on that napkin, forget about it. I'm not interested in a roomie tonight."

"Just read it." The man slid the napkin over

to her plate, and waited for her to read it.

Riley sighed and picked up the note. It read, in bold letters, ***Don't make a scene. We are leaving. NOW!!!*** Riley stared down at the napkin for a second or two more, then set it back down on the counter and took another drink of her beer.

"Huh." Riley was absolutely not in the mood to entertain this guy anymore and decided to show her cards. Grabbing her wallet, she threw a twenty dollar bill down on the counter and her badge down on top of it. "You just screwed up, bud. I'm FBI."

"I know." The man poked Riley's side with a handgun beneath the counter. "And I don't care."

Riley sighed again, though she had to admit that she did not foresee her night becoming this eventful. She took another drink of her beer and then waved goodbye to the waitress through the cook's window. Grabbing her badge, Riley dismounted the bar stool and made her way to the exit. The one time a guy pulled a gun on her in a diner, she'd left her gun back in the hotel room. The man kept behind her as the two crossed the road back towards the hotel.

No matter how quick or slow her pace, Riley noticed that the man kept the perfect distance behind her. He was professional, without a doubt. Once the two made it into her hotel room, and Riley clicked on the light, the man shut the door behind them and locked the bolt.

"Well, here's my room. Now what?" Riley peered back at the man with her hands to her sides. The man stepped back, but kept the gun on her, as he secured the curtains closed.

"Strip."

"Not gonna happen, bud."

The man rolled his eyes and cocked his gun. "Get over yourself. I'm not going to rape you. You're not my type. Now strip!"

"Then why?" Riley removed her suit jacket and began slowly unbuttoning her shirt.

"You're not supposed to be here, Agent; asking questions and digging around. Whatever you've discovered, it doesn't matter." Riley removed her shirt and left on her bra as she unzipped and began pulling off her jeans. "You're about to accidentally slip in the shower and crack your head on the linoleum. No one will know a thing."

An owl made a sound somewhere outside and the man momentarily looked toward the window. Riley took the opportunity as the only one she was going to get, throwing her jeans at the man's face and lunging toward his gun. Riley shoved the gun upwards as it went off and sent a slug into the ceiling. Riley forced the man backward into the wall, thrusting her knee up into his gut, and wrapping her arm around his to secure the gun. The gun went off two more times, shooting holes in the floor, as Riley struggled to gain control of it. She sent an elbow back into the man's jaw and bent his wrist backward until the gun fell from his hand. Riley went to grab it, but the man grabbed her by the arm and pulled her back around.

"You're going to regret that." Blood was dripping from his mouth, as he stared down at her with a fire in his eyes. Riley met his stare, didn't flinch.

"Bring it."

The man grunted in anger, rearing his head back, and then slamming it forward to smack her square in the forehead. Riley stumbled backward a step or two before the man grabbed the back of her neck and brought her back to dig his fist into her ribcage. She spat blood as she tried to breathe, but the man hit her in the chin with an uppercut that sent her falling back against the dresser with a large mirror attached on top it. The man grabbed her by the throat, lifted her off the ground, and slammed her body down atop the dresser. He stood over her, choking her, breathing heavily as he tried to finish her off right there and then.

"I didn't want it to down like this." He

tightened his grip as he spoke through clenched teeth. "But if you want to play this little game, I'll play."

"Screw the game," Riley grunted as she reached up for him.

Riley grabbed his head with both arms and brought her knee up to his temple. She kneed the side of his face a few times until his grip on her throat loosen. She quickly swatted his hand off her neck, punched him in the throat, and then grabbed the side of his head and slammed his face into the mirror. The man stumbled back away from her, as Riley rolled off the dresser and landed on the floor among the glass shards of the broken mirror. The man stumbled towards her as she crawled along the floor. Riley grabbed the base of tall lamp and swung it around to hit the man in the jaw. As he hit the wall and grabbed his head, Riley dove for the bed and dug her hand under the right pillow. Grabbing her gun, Riley spun around and fire one bullet. The man fell to his knees, a hole in the cheek just below his left eye, and face planted on the floor as pieces of his brain dripped from the splatter on the wall behind him.

Riley fell back against the side of the bed and caught her breath. She could hear someone yelling for the police outside. She pointed her gun towards the door, waiting to see if the man had any reinforcements coming to avenge him. When no one came, she sighed and put down her weapon. Standing up, she wiped the blood from her mouth and began putting her clothes back on.

Once she was dressed again, Riley rolled the man over and dug around in his pockets until she found his wallet. When she found nothing in it but cash, she returned to his jeans until she found his keys. Grabbing her gun, Riley left the hotel room and went searching for his car in the parking lot. As she clicked the button on his keychain, a black Dodge Charger blinked its lights in the corner of the lot. Riley ran over to it and opened the passenger door. When she found nothing in the glove compartment, she got out and headed for the trunk. Popping it open, Riley found a briefcase to be the only item inside.

The briefcase contained copies of Riley's flight itineraries, her rental car agreement, and current license. There were pictures of her leaving the airport, pulling up to Summerhill, and entering the facility. Searching the pockets of the case, Riley found a clip-on badge and flipped it over to read it.

"Adam Lepp, security for Reynolds Pharmaceuticals. Dammit!" Riley grabbed shut the trunk and ran over to her car.

Grabbing an additional handgun from the trunk, she stuffed a few loaded magazines in her pockets and donned her bullet-proof vest. She then returned to the Dodge Charger, hopped in the front seat and sped out of the parking lot and down the road towards Summerhill.

"This is Special Agent Riley Harper," Riley screamed into her phone as she stomped down on the gas pedal. "SCID: alpha-six-delta-five-two. I need the Maine branch to send a helicopter to the Summerhill Asylum with a backup team immediately. Agent and Informant are under attack!"

7 UNDER FIRE AT THE FUN HOUSE

Northern Maine, Near The Canadian Border

Riley swerved the car off the main road and onto the drive towards Summerhill. As she approached the entrance gate, she saw the broken glass and a guard hanging halfway out of the window, his blood dripping to the ground. Riley slammed her foot down on the gas pedal and crashed through the gate. She saw no one on the lawn, heard no sirens, and nothing about the building seemed disturbed. With the exception of the front gate guard, no one would suspect that the facility was under attach.

Riley stepped from the car and began to jog toward the front door. She released the magazine from her Beretta and verified that it was full. Shoving it back inside, Riley pulled back the slide and let it go; bullet in the chamber. Stepping through the door, Riley scanned the lobby. The receptionist had probably gone home before the attack, but there, in the center of the lobby, Nurse Pine laid across the floor in a puddle of blood. Riley stood over her and sighed as she bent down and grabbed the keycard from the bloodied coat.

Running down the main corridor, Riley could see flashing lights through the window of the secured door leading to the three wings. Making her way through, Riley found herself in the middle of absolute chaos. Light fixtures hung from the ceiling, bullet holes riddled the walls, heaps of burning patient documents and bodies filled the hallway. While some of the bodies were clearly patients, and others looked to be staff members, some looked like they were more likely part of the attack party; covered in black body armor, with faceless black helmets.

As Riley made her way towards the entrance of the second wing, she noticed movement toward the far end of the corridor; near the entrance to Wing Three. Nurse Pine had said that these criminals were of the less violent variety, but that could mean any number of things. Assault, rape, battery and other crimes could be considered "less violent" when compared to flat out murder. Either way, Riley could see that the door to Wing Three was open and a couple faint outlines were moving toward her through the smoke. The men appeared to be patients as they whispered to each other and began to spread apart to either side of the hall.

"Stay back! Don't make me shoot!" Riley raised her weapon towards them, more to show she meant business than anything. The two just crouched down and giggled, but continued to move toward her. Now at the intersection between the corridor and Wing Two, Riley looked up at the convex mirror on the wall and noticed two bodies begin to rise up from the floor behind her. Riley clenched her teeth and cursed to herself; the patients had staged an ambush.

"Get the bitch!"

Riley swung her arm around to point the barrel at the first of the two men lunging toward her from behind. She fired two rounds into the man's chest before moving to aim at the second man. Before she could get a shot off, a fifth man, who had been lying on the floor just next to her, tackled her from the side. Riley was slammed into the wall with such force that she accidentally dropped her weapon. The man laughed and growled as he picked her up and threw her to the floor. Another one of the men grabbed the gun and pushed himself on top of her.

"Now you're going to be a good little girl, or things are going to get nasty!" The man sniffed the barrel of the gun and laughed as he pointed it towards her face. Unable to reach her second gun, Riley lay still.

The man began to undo his pants as the other three men stood around him like hyenas looking to steal his score. The man looked up to see this and started swinging the gun around.

"Back off, you bastards, she's mine! You wait your turn!"

Riley took the opportunity to reach up quickly and grabbed the man's gun hand. Quickly wiggling her legs free, Riley pulled the man's arm down towards her as she wrapped her legs around his arm and neck. Locking one foot behind her other knee, Riley squeezed as hard and quickly as she could, trapping the man in a triangle choke. As he lost consciousness, he dropped the gun, and Riley quickly grabbed it and kicked the man off her.

Another man moved in to grab her, but she quickly shot him in the knee and scrambled backwards until she could get to her feet. The man screamed and he went down in pain, and the final two began to back away. As they started to run back towards the end of the corridor, Riley bolted for the door to Wing Two. Sliding in the keycard, she opened the door and quickly slammed it behind her, securing it shut.

Turning around, Riley noticed the hall mirrored the corridor. A night janitor lay dead on the floor, the overhead lights were flickering on and off, and the everything seemed to be turned over and spread across the floor. Just as she began to make her way down a section of the wing, the lights went out complete, and she was left alone in the dark.

"Great," she said, as she realized she didn't have a flashlight on her. A few seconds passed and the emergency lights kicked on. Riley took a breath and then cut it short when she heard something behind her.

"Get down, Agent Harper!"

Riley turned to see a tall figure, dressed in black body armor, aiming an UMP-45 submachine gun in her direction. Suddenly the figure was tackled to the floor by another man, and knocked unconscious when the man on top threw his elbow against the assailant's headgear. Riley trained her weapon on the man, as he stood up slowly with his hands raised.

"I don't want to say I told you so, but well, I kinda did."

Riley sighed as she lowered he handgun. "Shut up, Pierce. We need to get you out of here. There's a helipad on the north side, and I have a chopper inward bound."

Eugene knelt to pick up the submachine gun as he turned and smiled back at Riley. "Oh, you're welcome, no problem. No need to thank me or anything."

Riley rolled her eyes. "Do you even know how to use that thing?" She cautiously watched as Eugene flipped the gun to its side and pulled back the slide to check the barrel.

"Do I know how to use what? Oh, the gun?" Eugene released the slide, turned back to the armored figure on the floor, and sprayed the body with several rounds of ammunition. Eugen turned back and faked a confused expression in Riley's direction. "No, Agent. These gizmos are incredibly hard to understand."

"Right." Riley grabbed him by the arm and started to escort Eugene down the hall. "How many are there on the premises?"

"I've only seen three, but I put those down. I don't know how many else are here."

"We'll never make it to the helipad if we continue this way. We need to get to the common room and cut across the court yard."

The two ran down the hall toward the common room, passing cell after cell of one dead body after another. Riley figured whoever called for this attack wanted the entire place swept. They had confirmed that Eugene had spoken with her, but that could have only led them be that his story could have been told to anyone with ears in the facility. As they passed another cell, a patient called out for their help.

Eugene stopped and turned toward the bleeding man on the floor, but Riley pulled him back and pushed him forward down the hall.

This wasn't the time to play hero. She needed Eugene alive, if only to find out what the hell was going on, and that meant that they couldn't stop. As the two reached common room, Eugene stopped in his tracks, and Riley looked past him to see three armed men in the same armored attire, waiting across the room.

"Get down!" Riley shoved Eugene to the floor behind a sofa and dove down after him as the space around them was suddenly filled with bullets whizzing by. The two kept low as the bullets passed overhead and obliterated the bookcase in front of them. "Shit! We're pinned down!"

"Great observation, Agent!" Eugene threw an annoyed look her way as the two waited for a break in the shooting. When it came, and the sound of magazines being ejected, Riley and Eugene swung their arms over the sofa and opened fire. The attackers took cover, reloaded, and quickly returned fire. Riley and Eugene ducked back down low as they prayed the couch would hold for just a moment longer.

Suddenly Riley heard a zapping sound and turned to peer through a hole in the sofa. In the middle of the room, an ball of electricity began to form over the black circle she had noticed earlier on the floor.

Strings of electricity then began to climb towards the ceiling as a bright blue light encompassed the room. When the light vanished seconds later, Riley's eyes widened in amazement as she saw a figure knelt down on one knee in the center of the room; a short-haired girl, dressed in a skin-tight tactical suit, holding long daggers in each hand..

"Crap! Crap! Crap!" One of the assailants began to back away, as the other two stepped forward and raised their weapons once again.

"Shoot her! Shoot her!"

The girl bolted towards the aggressors, extending both arms as she released both daggers into the air. The daggers flew a short distance until they each met their marks and dug their way deep past the body armor. As the two men fell, the girl was already flying past them as she hit the third armed goon head on. Taking away his weapon, the girl stood up over him and pointed it down. As the trigger man reached out in protest, and begged through his faceless black face shield, the girl fired off a couple rounds into the helmet and stepped away.

"It's her. That's Juliet."

Riley broke her gaze and looked at Eugene. He was talking to himself as he counted how many bullets he had remaining. Riley ejected her magazine and grabbed another one from her pocket. "It's really here. She's actually here."

"Stay down, and stay put." Riley chambered a round as she stood and aimed her weapon at the girl. "Drop the gun! Do it now!"

"We don't have time for this. There will be more coming any second." The girl lowered her gun and slowed turned towards them. "Eugene? Are you all right?"

"I'll kill you!" Eugene shot up and raised his gun to fire. Riley quickly grabbed Eugene's arm and pushed it away as the shot fired.

"Not now, Pierce!"

The girl remained standing, unscathed, and raised her hands. "I'm only here to ensure your safety."

Just then a string of bright lights appeared in the courtyard and three more assailants stepped into view.

"We have to move, Eugene!" Riley grabbed his arm and pulled him down the hall as the attackers opened fire, shattering the windows and sliding glass door. Juliet appeared to stay behind to combat the gunmen, but soon appeared beside Riley as the three sprinted down the hall toward the north connecting corridor. Juliet ran past them and launched herself toward the secured door, shoulder first, breaking it off its hinges as she fell through to the corridor. Juliet opened fire, gunning down two more aggressors down the hall.

"There! Get through that exit," Riley shouted as she fired a few rounds down the hallway behind them. The three broke through the exit door and out into the night air. They ran as fast as they could for about a hundred feet before Riley looked up to see a helicopter and three FBI agents waiting for them; dressed in tactical armor packing large fully automatic rifles. "Everybody get down!"

"Assets clear! Open fire!"

The three hit the ground hard as the soldiers opened fire on the assailants pouring out of the facility. The shooting went on for what felt like forever as Riley and Eugene hugged the earth and stared at each other. Eugene was smiling with excitement, and Riley couldn't help but eventually smile back. When the firing ceasing, Eugene and Riley were helped to their feet.

"Where's the girl?" The third FBI agent scanned the area as Eugene and Riley were escorted quickly to the helicopter. Juliet was nowhere to be found.

"It doesn't matter! Let's get out of here," called one of the other agents as they all ran for the chopper. As soon as they were all on board, weapons trained on the asylum's exit door, the helicopter quickly rose up into sky and began it flight over the surround forest. Riley was handed a pair of headphones as one of the other agents signaled for her to talk through the attached microphone.

"Thanks for the help, fellas!" The other two agents each made a gesture back, but kept their rifles pointed out the windows. "I need to be patched into my supervisor, Agent Fischer, right away. It's urgent!"

"Negative, ma'am." The agent in the middle shook his head. "You've been reassigned."

"Reassigned," Riley screamed back at the agent, leaning forward to look him in the eyes. "What the hell are you talking about?"

"That's all I'm authorized to say, ma'am." The agent reached up and turned off the overhead cabin light, and leaned back in his seat. "We'll be at our destination in about an hour. Director Locke will fill you in on the details when we arrive."

"Director Locke?" Riley raised her eyebrows in shock. "Han Locke?"

The agent nodded, but didn't say anything

119

more. Riley sat back in her seat and wondered just what she had gotten herself into. The agent couldn't have been talking about the same person. Han Locke was a former decorated agent, last seen being shipped off to a secret prison somewhere for committing treason against the agency and the entire United States. If he was involved, then this was truly enemy territory. She had no idea what would be waiting for her when they landed, and the idea of it scared her more than what they just survived back at Summerhill.

8 THE CHANGE

Somewhere Under Ground, Nebraska

Officer Peter Drake sat on the floor against the wall of his cell, still in his combat boots, uniform pants, and his bloodied white t-shirt. A plastic tray of muck sat on the floor before him; he'd rather eat the processed garbage from elementary school lunch days. The cell had four walls of shiny chrome, a chrome plated toilet built into the wall, and a bed with mattress barely as thick as a piece of cardboard. The rest of the room was bare and cold.

He had lost track of the time and had absolutely no idea how many days he'd be trapped there. It couldn't have been many, but the lights never turned off, he wasn't given three meals a day, and there was nothing else that happened on the regular for him to judge the passage of time. He felt weak and tired, but he tried to avoid sleep as much as possible; he was unable to escape the fear that he would not wake. Suddenly the door opened.

"Let's go! You're coming with me." In the door stood two black-clad guards, each holding shock sticks. One of the guards tapped his stick against the metal wall and it shocked Peter enough to get him up. "Good. Don't make us use these."

The two guards escorted Peter out of the cell, each holding one of his arms tightly. The hallway was just like the ones he had run down before; chrome plated in sections, cemented brick in other sections. It was as if only the necessary areas of this underground bunker had been renovated for modern use, but the rest was apparently efficient even in its obvious old age. After walking for some time, the guards brought Peter into another chrome plated cell, this one with a single metal chair in the middle, and left him there. Peter stood there for a moment, and then turned and grabbed one of the guards.

"That's it? A different room with a chair?"

The guard shoved Peter back and then pushed him down into the chair. "Shut up and sit down."

The guards left and closed the door behind them. This room was the same size as Peter's last, except it had nothing else in it but the chair. Peter looked up to see a camera mounted in the corner; that was new as well.

Moments later, the door opened again to reveal a single guard escorted a small, frail-looking girl into the room. The girl was wearing a hospital gown as her only piece of clothing. She looked to be a teenager, or possibly early twenties. Her stringy hair, bruised pale skin, and the fact that she seemed to be shaking uncontrollably, suggested that she had been down in this hole longer than he had. The guard shoved the girl into a corner of the room, where she immediately balled herself up and hid her face, before once again leaving the room and shutting the door.

"Hey, wait! What is this?" Peter got up from his chair and hit upon the door. When no one answered, he turned and slowly approached the shriveled girl in the corner. "Miss? Are you all right?"

"I'm so sorry, mister." The girl could barely speak as she croaked our her words and tried to dig herself deeper into the corner.

Peter knelt down beside her. "What could you have to be sorry about?"

He reached out and touched her shoulder, but the girl quickly swatted his arm away and crawled to another corner. She held an arm out towards him as she kept her face hidden.

"Don't! Don't come any closer! Stay away from me!"

Peter stepped back and held his hands up. "You don't have to be afraid. I'm not going to hurt you, miss."

"No," the girl whimpered as she slightly turned her face towards him, while still hiding behind her hair. "But I will hurt you."

"Oh, darling. I don't think you could hurt me." Peter chuckled, trying to lighten the mood. "There's nothing for to worry about."

"You don't understand! I don't want to, but I will hurt you." The girl held up her hand in front of her face, watching it shaking to an uncontrollable degree. Suddenly she fell down to her knees and reached out for Peter. "Please! You have to help me, mister!"

"Anything! Tell me what to do," Peter said as he crouched forward with a smile.

"Kill me!"

Peter backed away in shock.

"Please! You must kill me, before it's too late. It's the only way."

"Okay, I don't understand." Peter got up to his feet and started pacing around, looking back and forth from the girl. "Did they do something to you? Are you okay?"

"You're not listening!" The girl was screaming at the top of her lungs now. She slammed both her hands down on the floor, digging her nails in, and clawed deep groove into the chrome. "They injected me with something. I know what happens. It's coming, and you have to stop it now!"

"All right, miss. Now cut that out. You're kind of creeping me out over here." Peter tried to smile, hoping a bit of humor would lighten the overtly creepy mood, but he failed to even convince himself.

The girl stood, her bones seeming to crack, break, and pop all over her body.

"I'm creeping you out?" The girl smiled as her entire body vibrated. "I'm going to ripping your guts out in a few moments. Now kill me! Do it!"

The girl lunged for Peter, grabbing him by both arms, as her mouth foamed. Everything was moving so fast, but Peter swore her teeth elongated, her bones began to peek through her skin, and her hair seemed to slide off her scalp. The girl brought her face within centimeters of him, hissed, and then continued to repeat the same words over and over; first starting at a whisper and then escalated to a screeching scream.

"Kill me! Kill me now! *Kill me!*" Peter couldn't think of what else to do, so he slapped her hard across the face and threw her back into the corner.

"Stop this! Pull yourself together!"

The girl laughed as she turned away from her and ran her claw-like fingers through her hair. Suddenly the laughter stopped and Peter heard the girl emit a quiet growling sound, like a threatened cat. Peter stepped back as the girl grabbed bundles of hair and pulled until there was no hair left and her fingers simply began digging deep into her scalp. The girl ripped long strips of flesh out off and threw them to the floor.

She screamed and growled at the same time as she shed her hospital down and bent over on the floor. She arched her back as the bones of her spine ripped themselves free of the skin, stretching themselves out from her back. Her shoulders buckled and then enlarged as her mass doubled itself. The screaming and growling intensified as her teeth fell out of her mouth, replaced with long ragged fangs. Her left eye exploded as her right eyeball squeezed out of its socket, flying in Peter's direction.

Peter backed away as far as he could, screaming toward the camera. "What the hell is this? Help me! You've gotta help me!"

He doubted anyone could hear him as the girl was now emanating a choir's worth of shrieking, hissing, growling, and roaring sounds. As it turned to face him from its crouched state, no longer resembling anything close to a human, Peter knew he didn't have a choice.

Before the creature could make a move, Peter grabbed the metal chair and swung it down upon the creature's head. The creature reared its head back around and roared, as blood and goo dripped from every crevice of its body. Peter began to scream himself as he brought the chair down upon the beast again, and again, and again. Finally, the creature broke down before him, but Peter didn't give up. He stood over it, swinging the chair down a fifth time, a sixth time, and more as splats of blood coated him and the walls with every strike.

He didn't stop until his arms grew tired, and by that point the creature hadn't moved for some time. Peter dropped the chair to his side, and backed away from the body. Covered in blood and guts, Peter looked up at the camera, wondering who had been watching him, who had put him through this.

"Why? Why did you make me do this? Why did you make me do this," he screamed at the camera, the same words over and over, unsure what else to say. He ran to the door and punched it with all his might.

Bloodying his knuckles, he hit the door again and again with each fist. "Let me out of here! Let me out! I want answers!"

Suddenly a vent opened up above him and a thick colored cloud of some kind of gas began to spew into the room.

No, no, no, dammit, he thought, as he turned back to the door and hit it again and again. He choked on the tampered air as his legs gave out. He fell to the floor, fighting to stay conscious, but it was no use.

Peter felt his mind body betray him as he could no longer keep his eyes open. With his last sober breath, Peter wondered if this was the end, if this was truly how he died.

9 THOMPSON TEDDY BEARS

Undisclosed Location in Vermont

The helicopter had landed at a private airstrip somewhere in Vermont. Riley had been removed from Eugene as they were both placed in separate, armored, black-tinted SUVs. The caravan drove for another hour or two before pulling into a lot of abandoned warehouses. The vehicle came to a halt and the two people up front exited. Riley tried to open her door, but it was locked. She pounded on the glass separating her from the driver and passenger seats.

"Tell me where the hell I am, right now!"

The two didn't pay her any attention as they stepped out and shut the doors behind her. Riley tried the other door, but with no luck. She banged on the glass and yelled again. "Let me out of this damn truck!"

Finally, the door opened on the other side, and a tall Asian man in his fifties stepped in and sat in the seat across from her. Riley looked at her former mentor, Mr. Han Locke, and sighed as she fell back into her seat.

"What the hell do you want?"

The man stared at her in silence and then chuckled to himself. "You're just as snappy as you were before."

Riley didn't return his laughter. She hadn't seen him since he taught her at the academy years ago, and she could only imagine what shady deals he was involved in now.

"You've been assigned to my unit, Agent Harper."

"Bullshit. You're not with the Bureau anymore. You have no authority over me," Riley said as she leaned forward with a finger pointed at Locke.

"You're correct, I'm not with the FBI any longer. This may come as a shock, but neither are you; not anymore."

Riley leaned back and crossed her arms. "Not anymore? Just what did you do? Did you ghost me?" Riley had heard of agents going bad. Their deaths were usually faked or something before they were suddenly on ever agency blacklist labeled as a traitor. "Just who the hell do you think you are?"

"I'm your superior authority, Agent Harper, and my patience with your insolent attitude is wearing very thin." Locke was clearly no longer entertained by Riley's abrasiveness.

"Screw your patience. I'm not playing along until I get confirmation."

Locke stared at her, and she stared right back. Finally, he broke and pulled out his cellphone. He pressed a few keys, spoke into it, and then handed the phone to her. A video link was open, and there was Agent Fischer, sitting in his office in Omaha.

"Fischer! Is this for real? Am I really no longer with the FBI?"

"That's right, cupcake. Your stubborn ass belongs to him now. Play nice, Agent."

Fischer leaned forward and cut off the call, and Riley just sat there, wondering what to say next. She lifted her head and peered back at Locke. Clearing her throat, she handed back his phone.

"My apologies, director." Riley straightened her jacket, one of her nervous ticks, and sat up straight. "I was told you were locked away somewhere for treason."

"They lied." With that, Locke stepped out of the vehicle and left the door open. Riley followed him out of the car and towards one of the warehouses. There were no signs on the building, but the faint outline of an old one read *Thompson Toys*.

"Oh, don't tell me we're based out of a toy company."

"Like I said, Agent, I'm getting tired of that lip."

Locke led her through a side door to the warehouse. The inside was still filled with boxes of *Thompson's Teddy Bears* and other famous toys from the company. Riley remembered seeing a few of them at some department store back when she was young; it almost made her smile.

At the back of the warehouse, Locke tapped some digits into a keypad next to the door and then leaned forward. The keypad retracted, and a retinal scanner took its place. After a brief red light scanned his left eye, the keypad returned, and the door unlocked.

"Welcome, Director Locke."

The door opened on its own and led to an enclosed white room. After Locke and Riley stepped in, the door shut behind them, and the white room began to move.

"Quite a fancy elevator you got here, Boss," Riley said. Locke rolled his eyes and ignored her.

When the elevator came to a stop the door opened into a large room of computers, similar to pictures she had seen of NASA's control room. A large screen illuminated the room of fifty or so agents on computers. The screen had a globe in the middle with certain dots and stats by each, but what caught Riley's eye was the letters written across the top of the screen: *MORS*.

"Welcome to my division. I haven't named it yet, but it's a black operations joint task force of former FBI, CIA, NSA, DEA and a few foreign intelligence agencies. Its sole purpose, currently, is to find out as much information as possible on the terrorist shadow organization known as MORS."

"So I'm not crazy?" Riley said it more as a rhetorical question, but she needed to say it none the less.

"No, you're not crazy." Locke motioned for Riley to follow as he led her up some stairs at the back of the control room to a glass office overseeing everything. Riley took and seat and Locke shut the door. Sitting at his desk, Locke leaned back, put his hands in his lap, and looked at Riley. "All right. Ask your questions."

"If you knew about this, and Fischer knew about this, why was I told to take a hike when I brought it in?"

"This is still a youthful operation, and there's a lot of red tape before we take someone in. When we couldn't find anything to corroborate your story about the North Bend phone call, we figured we'd cut you loose and see if you turned up anything else. You've been under our surveillance since you left Omaha. You mentioned MORS to Agent Fischer, and so that was enough to get our attention."

"What do you know about MORS?"

Locke took out a folder and slid it across the desk to Riley.

"This is what we know so far. MORS was the Roman god of death, but we're unsure of the connection. We know that MORS is a multi-branched organization. We've heard chatter of The MORS Initiative, The Church of MORS, and The Hand of MORS. We don't know much more than that. We've located a cult gathering outside of Panama City that we believe is the Church of MORS, but we have yet to infiltrate."

Riley fingered through the folder at the data. "Really? You have a wannabe Jonestown cult and some random chatter, and that's it? How did you manage to build a task force around this?"

"I have my ways, and I know when something is worth pursuing."

"And what about the girl we saved in Seattle? She said she was injected with something."

Locke grabbed a remote and flicked on the monitor behind him. Pressing a button, he played a video of a mass autopsy of all of the victims of Harold Jensen.

"While you followed your lead in Maine, we procured the bodies of Jensen's victims. When you saved Jessica Davis, there was another body recovered from that meat locker, a Jennifer Hagert. Unlike the other victims found throughout Seattle, Jensen had not yet removed the spikes from Jennifer. While we were able to recover those, we found nothing else on the scene to suggest what Jensen had been injecting into those girls. It seems Jessica Davis was the lucky one out of the bunch.

"The bodies are being dissected at a microcellular level in our lab downstairs, along with the spikes. My guys have yet to come up with something that explains what they are exactly, as their chemical makeup doesn't necessarily lend to anything on the periodic table. We are keeping our distance from the

Davis family, as we'd like to avoid putting a target on her back. We did bug the house and are watching from afar. If she exhibits any medical conditions, or if someone shows up looking for her, we'll be on it."

"Good. In all the mess of searching for Peter, I haven't had time to give much thought to her," Riley said. "I appreciate you picking up the slack." Locke nodded. "Ok, boss, so I guess that leads us to the last question. What do we know about Eugene Pierce?"

"Oh, Pierce is a whole bag of fun. Turns out the Bureau has been watching him since he escaped that conviction. While there isn't an official file on him, we have a black file that fills in his five-year hiatus before he checked into Summerhill. I'll fill you in on that later. As to your theory that he's connected to MORS, I admit I thought it was a stretch at first. Clearly, now, I know that to be a mistake. He's locked in a lounge downstairs. We'll be talking to him soon enough." Locket pulled out a large thick rubber black envelope with a locked zipper on the top that looked like a secured bank money bag. "Before we go any further, I'm going to need you to fill the bag."

Riley sat there for a moment, confused. She grabbed the bag and read the tag. It had her FBI badge number, her personnel number, the serial numbers on both her handguns, and her headshot from the academy. The bag already contained her two guns and her file. She reached down her shirt and grabbed the beaded chain holding her badge. Taking it off, she held it in her hand. It symbolized everything she had worked for over the past decade. It defined her, as sad as that reality was to her. She had absolutely no life outside of this job for the past decade, and now she was giving it up. She looked up at Locke and then back at the bag. She quickly dropped in the badge, zipped the bag, and put it back on the desk.

"So. If I'm no longer with the FBI, what do you call this unit?"

Locke took the bag and threw it in a locked filed cabinet.

"Still working on that."

10 THE ALBATROSS

Somewhere Under Ground, Nebraska

Peter struggled to open his eyes as he clung onto the arm of the sofa chair he currently slouching in. He felt like he was fighting to wake from a thousand-year-old sleep. His head ached, but the rest of his body was completely unresponsive. He tried to focus his energy; if he could move one finger, then he would gradually try to move the hand, wrist, and arm. He could hear someone moving around the room. He focused on his eyelids again, desperately trying to inch them open. As they started to give way, he could hear glasses clinking nearby.

"Yeah. It's been a bad week for me, too."

Peter's eyes were halfway open now. He could see his body beginning to twitch awake, limb by limb.

His skin smelled of bleach, and he noticed he was now wearing nothing but a hospital gown. He was sitting in a luxurious leather chair, in the middle of a private lounge of some kind. There was a man standing at the bar. He had incredibly pale skin, shoulder-length brown hair, wrinkles for days, and a thick Polish accent. Peter tried to speak back at the man.

"Huh? What was that again?"

The man turned around and searched a tall wall of liquor bottles on display. Finding a red wine, the man brought it down, uncorked it, and poured himself a glass.

"Oh, you passed out from the gas. We had to clean you up after the mess you made of poor Shelly. That was her name, by the way; the girl you so brutally killed back there."

Peter found his strength and jumped to his feet. Almost immediately as he did so, however, he felt his blood rush to his head. His legs wobbled, his knees buckled, and a strong sense of nausea overtook him.

"Oh, don't try to stand yet. Be patient now. The gas isn't completely out of your system. It's best if you just sit and listen for a bit."

"Listen to what?" Peter collapsed back into his chair. "Who are you?"

"My name is Samuel Stoke, and I run this facility." The man took a glass of ice and put it under a water tap, filling it to the brim. Walking it over, he placed it in Peter's hand. Peter tried to resist it, but when he suddenly felt an overwhelming thirst within him, he quickly brought the glass to his lips. "I'm also the only reason you're not dead in a ditch somewhere. So mind your tone, Mr. Drake."

"What do you want from me, Mr. Stoke? What is this place?"

Stoke brought the wine to his face, took in a deep whiff of its fragrance, and smiled. He toasted Peter and then took a sip.

"You've stumbled upon something here, Mr. Drake, and it's mainly due to Mr. Jensen's dirty habits. He was supposed to be quietly gathering subjects to test our formula on, but instead, his lust for underage girls led to him making reckless decisions." Stoke took another sip as Peter stared back at him. "Don't dwell on it. I got tired of snatching locals here in Nebraska, so I sent Jensen and some others to different locations for testing.

"On the upside, it appears his last victim has been released to her family with no reported side effects to Mr. Jensen's injection. So it's not a total loss."

Stoke grabbed a remote and turned on one of the several monitors on the wall behind his desk on the other side of the room. The monitor flickered, and then the rest did as well, to show all rooms within the Davis family home. One highlighted, and expanded until the wall of monitors showed one image—Jessica Davis working on her homework in her room.

"We will recover her later, when the news coverage has died down."

"Why? What could you possibly want from a teenage girl?" Peter downed the rest of the water and tried to sit up in his chair.

"We'll circle back to that." Stoke flipped off the monitors, grabbed his glass, and sat down in a chair across from Peter. "You know, the leadership wanted you dead, but I saw something in you. Especially when you bashed in little Shelly's skull."

"Tell me about the M.O.R.S. Initiative." Peter leaned forward, anxious to get this chat over with. "What kind of circus are you running here, Mr. Stoke?"

"Circus? Ha!" Stoke spit up a little of his wine and quickly dabbed at the droplets on his shirt with a handkerchief. "Hardly, though it can be quite a freak show at times."

Stoke walked over to the sink and wet his shirt a bit, trying to combat the wine stain. As he did, Peter took the opportunity to look around the room. The architecture suggested they were still underground, as the walls looked as if they could withstand a heavy surface blast. Stoke's lounge was on one side, and his office on the other. A private elevator services the room, and the fourth wall was made of windows overlooking a vast bay about three stories deep. From where Peter was sitting, he couldn't see what was going on in the bay, but he could see lights flickering and assume it was some time of massive workshop or lab.

"I like you, Peter, and since we have some time here, and I don't often get the chance to chat with outsiders, I'm going to give you a little speech." Stoke walked over with a carafe and refilled Peter's water glass.

"Humanity is at its weakest moment, Peter. We've overtaken this planet, but only to pullet it. We've ceased our efforts to better ourselves, to become greater than our previous generations. We've abandoned our roots as pioneers. We've become lazy and bored without existence, and in that boredom, we've become weak and afraid.

"We no longer, as a race, reach for the stars, for advances in medicine, anatomy, transportation or travel. We tell fictitious tales of space and the new frontier, and yet we spend all of our money and resources on the next model of cellphone. There are too many of us in numbers, and not enough of us with vision. Quantity over quality, you could say. The world lacks visionaries, people willing to stand against the tide, against the oppression of the mind. The fierce among us are fading out of existence to give way to the submissive and weak.

"We have allowed society to rule over reason. We let them dictate what we say, what we think, what we believe, and what we strive to achieve, all in the name of morality. We bastardized those who attempted to achieve more. Paracelsus, Oppenheimer, Lysenko, the Nazi experiments, the Roslin Institute. Did you know that the Rolin Institute successfully cloned a sheep over two decades ago? Two decades, Peter! Most have forgotten because the science was shamed and banned.

"My father, William Stoke, despite his ties to Poland, was recruited by Adolph Hitler himself to conduct human testing that even his top men would refuse to do. I can admire a man like that. Someone willing to stand against the rest of the world, and dispense of worthless lives in the pursuit of something greater.

"If the human race ever evolved to begin with, we've come to a standstill. Mother nature attempts to burn us off, like a fever does a virus, but she's moving too slow. So a few of us got together awhile back, and realized the potential we shared. If the world wasn't willing to move forward, we would provide the push. We pooled our resources together, split off into factions, and initiated a process to bring about our will upon humanity. The M.O.R.S. Initiative is the answer to mother nature's problem, the cure to the virus that is us.

"I have never been one for politics, and I'll never admit that I'm not all that bright on general business operations. I do, however, know my science. What you saw in Seattle was just a taste of what we are working on here. The formula is made up of something the United States discovered about a decade ago and burrowed away from the public eye. It is, how best to say this, not of this earth.

"When I began breaking it down, all those years ago, I found that it had elements that could force our race into the next era of evolution. Due to its abrasive qualities, it won't match with most humans. Thus, the lucky ones, those like little Jessica Davis, are considered genetically to be the chosen few, the better among us.

"So when I brought my findings to our little group, this facility was built to serve our needs. Of course, you witnessed one of our other inventions as well: teleportation. I admit, I've used that more as a tool than as a revelation, but it is what it is. So as you can see, you've stumbled upon something years in the making, and we can't just let you leave and go tell everyone, now can we? Especially when there are so many out there who would bring in their laws, and their rule books, and their sanctions to stop us from doing what it is we must do.

"Do you know what an Albatross is, Mr. Drake?" Stoke took a sip of his wine as Peter pondered whether or not this was a trick question.

"It's a big-ass bird, right?" Peter attempted to sound as sarcastic as possible.

"Haha, yes. There is, however, a secondary, older definition. An albatross is an obstacle, something that stands in the way; on obstruction to progress. We, the human race, are the albatross to our own selves. Our refusal to evolve into greater beings, hinders our existence an purpose. There are few among us with the spark to take us to the next stage, and those fierce individuals will thrive once the M.O.R.S. Initiative has cleared away the muck."

"So, what then? Your plan is to thin the herd? To obliterate the human race?"

Stoke looked down at his glass and sighed. "Yes. We are here to destroy the human race, in order to save those who are worthy and force us into the next evolutionary state of being." Stoke took one more sip of his wine and pressed a button on his desk. "Now, like I said, I can't have you going off to tell your friends about what you've seen here. I would just have them take you down to the cellar and put a bullet in you, but with the display you put on while taking care of Shelly, I think I have something better suited for you."

At that moment, the elevator opened and two guards stepped into the room. Peter tried to stand, knowing that this would likely be his last chance to defend himself, but the effects of the gas still had a hold on him. The guards helped him to his feet and carried him to the elevator.

"What is this? What are you going to do to me, Stoke?" Peter attempted to struggle, but it was no use.

"Don't worry, Mr. Drake. It will be painful at first, but sooner than later you won't remember a thing." Samuel Stoke raised his glass as Peter was put in the elevator.

"To you, Mr. Drake, and to the future!"

11 REAL TALK

Thompson Toys, Somewhere in Vermont

Eugene Pierce paced back and forth in the room that they had placed him in. The room had a television set that didn't work, a phone that didn't work, a couple couches that felt like they were made of broken pieces of brick, and the most blindingly bright florescent lights known to man. There was a clock on the wall. Eugene knew that it displayed the wrong time, but he could keep track of the passage of time at the very least.

After four hours had passed without a peep, Eugene went to the door and pounded on it.

"Hey! Anyone! I need to use the rest room!" No answer. " You want me to go in here? Really?"

149

After a moment, Eugene heard a lock release, and the door opened. A young, clean-cut man in a black suit stood on the other side. He didn't say a word. He didn't express any kind of emotion on his face. He simply stretched out his arm, and signaled Eugene which way to walk. Eugene stepped through the door and walked in front of the agent. As abruptly as possible, Eugene stopped and turned back towards the room, bumping into the agent.

"Oh, I'm sorry, I forgot something in the room." Eugene's right hand gracefully invaded the agent's pant and jacket pockets until he found the two items he needed; a cellphone, and a security badge.

"You can get it later! Move!" The agent, none the wise, pushed Peter back in the proper direction until they reached the rest room. The agent remained outside while Eugene went in; now that he was here, he found he did, in fact, need to use the facilities. After washing up, Eugene reentered the stall and took out the cellphone, dialing the only number he had memorized since he left the manor ten years ago.

"Hello? This is Theodore Leboush."

Mr. Leboush was the only person that visited Eugene after the trial. While Eugene was deciding what to do with his life, what he could do with all the paparazzi watching his every move, Mr. Leboush would visit and assure him that he and his assets were in good hands. Leboush was a department head within Reynolds Pharmaceuticals, an old college of both of Eugene's parents, and so he was the closest thing Eugene had to a guardian.

"Do you know who this is, Theo?" Eugene waited through the silence, still unsure if this was the best idea.

"Eugene? Is that you? Is that really you, buddy?" There was excitement in Leboush's voice that Eugene couldn't quite tell if it was genuine or not.

"Am I your buddy, Theo? After last night's events, I don't know if that's true anymore." Eugene heard pounding on the door. He knew the agent was getting impatient. Eugene covered the phone and responded. "Give me a minute! I've been locked up in there all night, for goodness' sake!"

"What are you talking about, Eugene? Are you still at Summerhill?"

Eugene thought deeply about what he might say next. Obviously the phone call alone verified that he was alive, but he was sure that whoever sent the men to kill him would know about their failure any way.

"Summerhill was attacked last night, Theo. Men came in to kill me." There was a silence on the other side. "Tell me you don't know about it."

"Are you sure that's what happened? I mean, five years in a place like that could play tricks with your head."

"I know what I saw, Theo. The woman that saved me has proof that they were dispatched from Reynolds Pharmaceuticals. Don't try and deny it." Another moment of silence passed. At this point, Eugene was all but certain that Theo was not alone.

"Where are you now, Eugene? We can talk this out. Clearly, there's been some kind of mistake here. You're the son of Ronald and Jane Pierce. You're family to this company."

Eugene knew this was a mistake, but he figured the agent's cellphone had to have some kind of protection from being traced, so he had no intention of hanging up just yet.

"Tell me where you are, Eugene. I'll come get you myself."

****

When Director Locke was finished giving Riley the tour of the place, and Riley had secured her new credentials and sidearm, the two had returned to the main operating room to discuss next steps. Riley was impressed, to say the least, at level of activity she witnessed on just one of the fifty computer screens currently active in the room. The access was completely unlimited and no form of privacy existed as a barrier from this setup. Still, with all the firewalls and red tape dispensed with, the people in this room couldn't find any tangible, actionable evidence of MORS.

Suddenly, the a red light came on above one of the computer stations, and the attendant stood and signaled Director Locke to come over. Riley followed.

"What do we have, agent?" Locke and Riley peered over the agent's shoulder at the computer screen.

"We've intercepted a call to someone high on the totem pole at Reynolds Pharmaceuticals, a Mister Theodore Leboush. From what I can tell, the conversation is in regards to last night's event at Summerhill."

"Triangulate the origin of the call. I want to know who's talking to Leboush."

The agent opened a satellite protocol program and entered in a code granting access to the software's search parameters. Within moments, the agent had his answer.

"Uh, it's coming from here. The signal is emanating from our location!"

Director Locke immediately unholstered his sidearm and headed towards the stairs.

"Let's go, Agent Harper! I believe we need to have a chat with Mr. Pierce."

Riley grabbed her gun and bolted after him.

****

"You must me naïve to turn myself over to the company who tried to kill me," Eugene said. "Did you kill my parents too?"

"Of course not, Eugene," Leboush replied. "You know how close I was to your parents. Their deaths were equally tragic and the company has wanted nothing more than to ensure your happiness. Now tell me where you are, Eugene. I can be there within the hour."

Suddenly the bathroom door broke off its hinges as the room was invaded by Director Locke and several men. One of them took the phone, hung up the call, and ejected the sim card.

"What do you think you're doing, Mr. Pierce?" Director Locke grabbed Eugene's arm and escorted him out of the room.

As they entered the hall, Eugene shrugged Locke's grip off him and backed away. The men around Locke raised their weapons as Riley simply watched.

"Really?" Eugene grabbed the nearest gun, twisted around and elbowed the agent in the face. Tossing the gun at the next nearest agent, Eugene dropped to the floor and kicked the legs out of another agent. Rising to uppercut the final agent, Eugene stood in front of Locke while the men all laid on the floor in pain. "You lock me in a room for five hours and ask me what the hell I'm doing! I appreciate the helivac from Summerhill, but I will not be held prisoner."

"I apologize for our inconsiderate behavior, Mr. Pierce, but that does not warrant you calling the enemy without regard to the security or secrecy of this base."

Eugene rolled his eyes as he turned and helped up one of the agents. "Oh, don't give me that. A black operations unit like this probably has at least three redundancies for my phone call. If they were tracing it, they likely thought we were in another state on the opposite side of the nation. Am I right?"

Locke stood there and looked down at Eugene for a moment before he checked his watch and turned to walk back down the hallway.

"Please follow me, Mr. Pierce. We are about to have a visitor that I will need your assistance with."

****

Outside of the Thompson Toys warehouse, a taxi pulled up. Once she paid the driver, Juliet Cubro stepped from the car and surveyed the area. It mattered not if this was a trap. Juliet was simply intrigued by the invitation and thought it might be worth her time to at least look into what they had to say.

As the cab drove off, Juliet approached the warehouse and through the front door. She barely walked fifty feet into the warehouse before she heard the shouts and weapons cocking. As she was commanded from several different people to drop down to her knees and interlace her fingers, a dozen or so red dots appeared on her chest. She complied with their commands and waited as the men surrounded her.

"Is this really all that necessary, guys?"

****

"I really don't see how I could be any help to your unit here, Mr. Locke." Eugene sat next to Riley, opposite Director Locke in a conference room. "Like I said, I'm grateful for your assistance, but I'd rather just be on my way."

"Don't cut yourself short, Mr. Pierce. You aren't as useless as you appear." Locke slid a folder over toward Eugene. "As you can see from that file, you were never as far off the grid as you thought. It seems you took a few years of martial arts training before you spent a short time actively seeking out aggressive criminals on probation. Were you just doing your civic duty to ensure the public's safety, or were you trying to test your skills against the ruthless?"

"So you've been playing big brother. How surprisingly cliché of a government lapdog. I still don't see what I could know about your MORS investigation." Eugene closed the file and tossed it back on the table.

"They just tried to kill you, Mr. Pierce. Certainly that must be worth something."

The three sat in silence.

"That's it? You're banking on this guy to connect the dots for you? He's been locked up in a nut house for five years!" Riley was clearly annoyed to find that such an impressive unit was based on such little actual intel.

"Yes, we are, Agent Riley; him, and one other person." Locke's phone beeped, and he checked the message and smiled. "It appears Ms. Cubro has just now arrived."

"Excuse me?" Eugene shot to his feet and slammed his hands down upon the table. "What the hell is she doing here? She killed my father! She tried to kill me! She's the reason for…everything!"

Director Locke rose from his chair and lifted his hands to try to calm Eugene down. "She clearly has some knowledge that could be valuable to us. When I saw that her presence at Summerhill was to ensure your safety, I thought it might be worth reaching out to ask for her help. We flooded the dark web with a coded invite for her to find, and she agreed to a meet. I do, however, understand and sympathize with your perspective." Locke clicked a button on a remote, and the monitor behind him blinked on to show Juliet Cubro sitting in an interrogation room. "For this reason, I've arranged for you to meet with her first."

"You what, now? You expect me to go in there and talk to her, and not kill her?"

Locke shrugged and put his hands in his pockets. "It was her only prerequisite." Locke motioned for an agent to enter. "My agent will escort you to the room. We will be watching in case she tries anything."

Eugene stormed out of the room, but not before Riley stopped him and placed a hand on his shoulder. She nodded encouragingly, and Eugene continued on his way. As he followed the agent toward the interrogation room, Eugene tried to think of what to say. He had dreamed of hunting her down for the past ten years. Every night he had dreamed of exacting his revenge upon her in one way or another; the only exceptions would be the few nights that he would dream of being intimate with her, as he never fully had gotten the chance to be. Now he was about to be alone with her, for the first time since the night his father died, and he was without an idea of how he should proceed.

****

The agent opened the door, and Eugene entered the interrogation room, and sat down at the table, across from Juliet. He thought for a moment not to look at her, but he found himself staring at her and dissecting every piece of her appearance. Save for her short dark hair, she appeared just as flawless and youthful as the day he had met her. She stared back at him, slightly waving while handcuffed to the table, and smiled.

"Hello, Gene."

Eugene's fist clenched under the desk at the sound of her voice. He knew that Director Locke and Agent Harper were likely on the other side of the two-way glass, watching his every move; his options here were limited.

"No, no, no. You do not get to start this." He could feel his emotions swell within him as he tried to stay strong. "Do you have any idea what you did to me? You killed my father in front of me! Then you left me. You really….screwed me up."

"I know." A tear escaped from Juliet's eye and ran down her face; it matched the one on Eugene's cheek. "I was anxious, and impatient that night. It was supposed to happen differently, and at a time when you would not be there to witness it. There are things you don't know about your family, Gene. I wanted to tell you, but it didn't go down that way."

The Pierce Manor, Bridgeport, Connecticut
10 Years Ago

Juliet and Mr. Pierce had just started another nightly game of chess as they talked about what she had learned from her internship that day.Eugene had left for a bike ride, and the staff had left for the night. Juliet was content with testing her chess skills again, but it was clear that Mr. Pierce was more interested in conversation for the evening.

"So tell me where you're from, Juliet." Mr. Pierce took a sip from his brandy glass and peered over the table to determine his next move.

"I grew up in Sarajevo, sir."

Ronald nodded, as if he had remembered that detail. "What kind of childhood did you have? I imagine it was quite complex to have developed you into such a smart young woman." Ronald moved a pawn and then sat back in his chair.

"I had no childhood, Mr. Pierce. I was raised in a cage." While it hadn't been an actual cage, it was a fairly close allegory to the true reality of her upbringing.

"That's...terrible, Juliet. Was it due to the recent civil war over there?"

Juliet went to move her knight, but ended up clenching it in her hand. She had not prepared to have this conversation that night.

"No, it wasn't. I was raised in a research facility built in the aftermath of the war. A company had swooped into the capitalize on the region's desperate state. In exchange for financial help in rebuilding the cities, the company was given some land and absolute privacy to do whatever they wished upon that land. Every day was the same. Same clothes, or lack thereof, same tests, same food, and same supplements. Do you know what drugs they gave me four times a day?"

"My goodness, I have no idea. What did they give you?" Mr. Pierce was no longer focused on the game and had put down his brandy glass.

"I never knew their exact chemical makeup, but the pill bottles and needle vials all said the same brand name: Reynold Pharmaceuticals." The more she spoke, the more Juliet knew this was the moment. She could not back out now.

"Oh, God, no. You can't be." Ronald had a look of shock upon his face, as if a revelation just occurred to him that pieced all of Juliet's story together. "You're from one of Samuel Stoke's facilities."

"You may be playing a lessor role, now that your wife is dead, but it doesn't make you innocent." Juliet reached beneath her shirt to grab the tactical knife tucked away in her pants.

"I know." Ronald's head dropped in dismay. "I never liked what Samuel did."

"But you certainly didn't care enough to stop it." Juliet continued to clench the knight in her hand, on the verge of breaking it.

"You don't understand, Juliet. I can explain." Ronald reached out to comfort Juliet, but she slammed her fist down upon the game table and knocked over the chessboard.

"Don't! You know why I'm here, you deserve this."

THE FIERCE ARE FADING

Ronald put his hands up in surrender and retracted back into his chair. "I'm so sorry, Juliet. I didn't know." Ronald showed deep remorse across his face, but Juliet was far beyond caring at this point. "I had no idea you were one of Samuel's."

"I belong to no one!" Juliet stood, knife in hand, and lunged at her target.

Thompson Toys, Somewhere in Vermont

"He knew about a facility, and that was enough to kill him?" Eugene knew it was more complicated than that, but he didn't know what else to say. He had known little to nothing about his father's business matters, and all of this was hitting him like a wave that he had no choice but to be taken under by.

"Yes, that's enough. They knew more than simply the facility's existence, but I don't have time right now to spell it out." Juliet reached to touch Eugene's trembling hand, but she couldn't reach with the handcuffs.

"What did they do to make you hate them so much?" Eugene knew he probably didn't want to know the ugly details, but it was all he could ask.

"One day I'll tell you." Juliet seemed to get lost in that thought for a moment, but then snapped out of it and peered back at Eugene. "Your parents were evil people, Gene. I'm sorry, but that's the truth."

****

The door opened, and Director Locke entered the room. Eugene looked up and realized that his time was up. He glanced at Juliet's somber, yet beautiful face one more time before standing and exiting the room. Director Locke shut the door and the sat down across from Juliet.

"Now that that's out of the way, I'm going to need you to bring something more to the table than a sob story, Ms. Cubro." Locke placed his sidearm on his lap beneath the table. "You're a world renowned assassin with more than thirty-five kills under your belt, not including the unfortunate bodyguards or henchmen that got in the way. To my knowledge, this is the first time any government official has seen you in person. You obviously have some similar abilities as the MORS agents. So the obvious first question is, how can I trust you?"

"Enemy of my enemy?"

Locke nodded toward the two-way glass, and an agent entered the room with a file folder of MORS documents, as well as some writing utensils and paper. The agent unlocked the cuffs and left the room.

"You're going to have to do better than that. Take a look at those documents and tell me something I don't know. Then we'll talk." Locke watched as Juliet scanned the documents, picked up her pen, made four dots, and then put it back down. Juliet slid the piece of paper over to Locke. Juliet had placed periods in between the letters to turn MORS into M.O.R.S.

"M.O.R.S. isn't just an ancient Roman deity. The letters actually stand for the initials of the last names of the four heads of the organization. I currently only know two of them; Samuel Stoke and the late Jane Reynolds."

Locke smiled at the revelation. These four dots marked the first real development in his investigation. "Why do you share similar traits to their agents?" Locke had still yet to loosen his grip on his sidearm.

"I escaped from one of their human testing plants at a young age. I have technology implanted in me that allows me some of the same abilities as their military members. When I accrued the skills to exact my revenge, I went after the Pierce family."

"Did you take the taxi here for the ambience? Why didn't you just teleport here, like you did with Summerhill?" Locke took notes as Juliet spoke. Being ambidextrous allowed him to keep his other hand's trigger finger ready.

"An implant within me allows me to teleport from any location, but I can only teleport to a receiving unit. Unless my target has a unit or, in Summerhill's case, I've arranged for a makeshift one to be installed, I cannot teleport there. I've found it to be more of a last resort escape option than an offensive tool in most cases." Juliet leaned back and Locke finished his notes. "I'm not going to give you a breakdown of the rest of my implants or abilities unless the time comes when it's necessary. While I don't know much more about M.O.R.S., why don't you tell me what you have and I'll try to fill in some of the blanks."

****

Riley left the viewing area for the interrogation room and went out into the hall to look for Eugene. She found him sitting against the wall a ways down the a nearby corridor. She waved the nearby agents away and sat down beside him. Eugene was clearly distraught, holding his head in his hands as he peered down at the tiled floor.

"You all right?" Riley plopped down to the floor next to Eugene and leaned her head back against the stone wall.

"Not really the day I expected."

Eugene kept a straight face, but Riley smiled a bit. She couldn't help but be intrigued by this break in his normal hard, sarcastic exterior. "I imagine not. Do you believe what she said?"

Eugene sighed and slapped his knees. He scratched his head as he searched for an answer. "My family used to go camping on some land my father owned an hour or two outside of Omaha. He liked to hunt there from time to time. It was the last night we were all together, before the crash. I knew they weren't happy, but they were trying for me." Eugene ran his hands back and forth over his pants. "They would argue late into the night about various problems with work, but always too vague for me to understand. I'd like to believe they were good people, but... There are too many reasons why I shouldn't."

"That's rough." Riley thought to pat him on the shoulder, but decided against it.

"The look in her eyes, I could see such a deep pain through her beauty. It's hard to deny her when she's sitting right in front of you."

Riley smirked at how lost Eugene seemed to be in all of it. "You sound like you're in love all over again."

Eugene dropped his head and smiled. "I don't really know if I ever stopped."

Riley went with her instinct this time and patted Eugene on the shoulder. She hopped back up to her feet and headed back down the hallway. Suddenly it hit her, and Riley stopped flat in her tracks and turned back to Eugene.

"Wait. Did you say your father had land outside of Omaha? As in Nebraska?"

12 SLEEPLESS

Seattle

"I swear! You'll pay for that!" Jessica Davis stood over her opponent, determination in her eyes, weapon in hand as she prepared to strike. With all her strength, she brought her pillow down upon her second best friend of all time and relished in the satisfaction as the pillow collided with the other girl's face. "Haha! Got ya!"

For the first time since the incident, Jessica had convinced her parents to take the night off and let her be. While they had left for a late night dinner and movie, Jessica was allowed to have her four closest friends over for game night. The girls had spent so much time worried that Jessica would hate them for dropping her off in that Taco Bell parking lot, but

Jessica wanted nothing more than to just spend time among friends, people not trying to get a sound bite, a picture, or catch her at a vulnerable moment.

Patricia, Chloe, Brittany, and Nicole were all in their favorite comfy pajama sets, hanging out in her room. While Nicole and Jessica went to battle on her bed with the largest pillows they could find, Patty, Chloe, and Brit were playing Monopoly on the floor as the mp3 player blared their favorite late night radio station. Patty rolled across the floor and grabbed her duffle bag.

"Look what I brought!" Out of the bag, Patty pulled a six-pack of wine coolers that she had convinced some middle-aged guy to buy for her at the convenience store down the street. The other girls began to shriek in excitement as each of them grabbed one.

"Give me one of those." Jessica twisted off the top of the bottle and attempted to down it as quickly as she could. The room filled with chants for her to chug the whole thing as Jessica fought to finish the bottle before gasping for air. The girls cheered when Jessica released the bottle from her lips and flipped it over to reveal that it was truly empty.

"Jessica is such a rebel!" Chloe laughed as she passed Jessica the final bottle. "You know, now that she's a mass murderer survivor celebrity and all!"

"Chloe!" Brit laughed as she smacked Chloe on the leg. "That's so bad!"

"Haha, Chloe! Screw it, I don't care." Jessica attempted to down the second bottle but suddenly felt as if something was wrong. She felt a sharp pain in her gut and felt the nausea hit her hard as she dropped the bottle and covered her mouth.

"Are you all right, Jess?" Nicole had a look of concern on her face.

"Ugh, no, I don't think so." Jessica, now teary-eyed due to the nausea and sheer pain flowing through her body, suddenly bolted toward the bathroom attached to her room. "I think I'm going to be sick!"

"Ha! Light weight!" Patty threw a pillow at Jessica as she ran to the bathroom. After the girls laughed for a bit, they heard a high-pitched shriek come from the bathroom followed by a thud.

"Oh, no! I hope she didn't fall over," said Chloe as she rose to her feet and headed toward the bathroom. "I'm going to go check on her."

Chloe knocked on the door as she pressed her ear against it. She could hear movement as well as sporadic crying coming from inside. Chloe slowly opened the door and peeked her head inside. Before she could ask if Jessica was all right, her eyes took in the sight of the blood-drenched walls, the broken toilet bowl, and finally the bloody mass in the tub, wrapped in the fallen shower curtain.

"What the hell?"

Before Chloe could back out of the bathroom, the mass in the tub jumped up onto the ceiling and then dove in her direction. Chloe screamed at the top of her lungs for all of about five seconds before her body was severed in half.

****

"Unit four to base. We've arrived at the Davis house."

Officer West and Officer Krueger exited their patrol car and made their way toward the front steps of the house.

"Isn't this the house of the girl that got kidnapped?" Officer Krueger held a flash light in one hand as he unbuckled the safety strap over his sidearm.

"Yes, Krueger." West followed suit as the two reached the front door. "Nice beard, by the way."

"Oh, can it, West. I'm still on special duty." Krueger knocked on the door a few times and waited. "I hate it, too."

"Seattle Police. Is anyone home?" West knocked on the door as well, but no one answered.

Twisting the knob, West found the door to be unlocked. The two slowly entered the dark house, flashlights fanning across the empty space. No one seemed to be downstairs, but there was a flickering light coming from somewhere upstairs. Suddenly, both officers heard a thud, followed by a rattling sound come from the floor above them. Both officers immediately took out their weapons and began to climb the stairs.

"This is the Seattle Police. We are coming up the stairs."

Each stair creaked just enough to raise every hair on Officer Krueger's arms. His weapon was fixed on the open space at the stop of the stairs, while his other hand crossed over his arm to aim the flash light on the same spot. Officer West was the first to reach the top of the stairs. He panned his flashlight up and down the hallway, finding that all doors were shut with the exception of the second one on the left; the source of the flickering light. He covered the other half of the hallway as Officer Krueger stepped towards the open door. Krueger quickly made his way to the opposite side of the open door and waited for West to join him. The two silently counted to three, and then both made their way into the room, weapons ready.

"Oh.....damn. Unit four to base, you need to get some backup out here now," Officer West spoke into his shoulder radio as he scanned the area.

The room was covered with the insides of what appeared to several teenage girls. The ceiling fan had at least one set of intestines hanging from it, blocking the light as the blades of the fan circled around and around. It did not appear as if any of the girls had been left in one piece. Heads, arms, legs, and so on were scatter across the room. As the flashlights panned the room, something moved in the corner.

"What is that thing?"

The creature rose from its crouched state, hissing as it presented its full mass to the officers.

"Oh, God help us. Shoot it, now! Kill it! Kill it!"

****

A small crowd of neighbors began to gather out in the middle of the street. The red and blue lights of the patrol car painted the Davis' house. Shouting could suddenly be heard from the house, follow by frantic gun shots that made the crowd scream in shock. The shots went on for only a minute or two, interspersed with sounds of broken glass, heavy thuds, and desperate screams coming from within the house.

Then the noises ceased all together. A few minutes went by until Officer West stumbled out of the front door, covered in blood. He fell to his knees on the porch as he reach for his shoulder radio.

"Unit four to base. We need…" West gasped for air he dropped his gun to the floor. "I need help. You gotta send someone. Officer down. I got an officer….down. Krueger's all in pieces, man. You gotta send someone…please."

13 INTO THE DEPTHS OF HELL

Thompson Toys, Somewhere in Vermont

"All right, we're back to Nebraska. Now both the FBI and my initial teams found nothing the first time. What's changed?"

Director Locke stood in front of the massive screen, currently displaying the state of Nebraska, in the main operations room with Riley, Eugene, and Juliet standing behind him.

Riley stepped forward and clicked a remote toward the screen. The map zoomed in on Dodge County, displaying all the property lines around North Bend, Nebraska.

"Eugene's family apparently owns land in North Bend, near the location where I last heard from Officer Drake. It's just too big of a coincidence to not warrant a second look."

"Miss Cubro?" Locke turned and looked at the assassin. "You have their technology. Are you able to locate their structures?"

"Only if I know approximately where it could be, within a few miles." Juliet raised her left forearm to reveal a computer display being projected from beneath her skin. "I did locate something beneath the surface, and already gave the data to your people. There's an old Strategic Air Command bunker and former missile silo that appears to have been erased from most records. The bunker wasn't on most public lists for obvious regions, but someone went above and beyond and wiped a bunch of higher clearance records as well."

"Then that's it. That's where Peter is, and that's where we find M.O.R.S." Riley stepped forward, next to Director Locke, looking at the screen. Locke continued to stare at the data for a moment, then looked at Riley. When he found whatever he was searching for in Riley's eyes, he turned to Juliet.

"Miss Cubro? Other than combat, what support can you offer?"

Juliet sat back in a chair, legs raised on a desk, twirling her knife. "I can bypass their firewalls and teleport in, ahead of your men, to one of their receiver units. I could give you a last second read before your breach, and take down a few men while I do it."

Locke nodded in approval. Eugene stepped forward, hand raised.

"I want in on this as well, Director."

Locke looked at him, and then over to Riley. Riley nodded in silent approval, and Locke smiled back at Eugene.

"Fine. I'm short on men either way. From what I see, you're capable enough to handle yourself. See the armory for gear."

Director Locke turned toward the rest of the agents in the room and pressed a button on the podium to connect to the base intercom system.

"All right, listen up. I want whatever floor plans we can come up with. They will have likely made some refurbishments, and may have even conducted a massive construction overhaul, but we would have a start. I want multiple breach strategies, with at least three solid entry points. I need a head count of all available agents, as well as a detailed summary of our weapons inventory. You've got one hour to come up with a game plan, people. Let's move."

"Gene!"

Everyone bolted in different directions while Juliet grabbed Eugene's arm and dragged him down a hallway. Shoving him against a wall, she put a finger on his chest and looked deep into his eyes. "You think I saved your ass so you can get killed the next day?"

"Why did you save me, then?" Juliet stepped back, almost surprised by the question. "How did you know I was in danger anyway? After ten years, why do you care?"

"Don't you know? I'd do anything for you." Juliet dropped her head and sighed. Then, before Eugene could process what she had said, Juliet stepped forward and kissed him deeply.

When they broke, Eugene didn't know quite what to say. "Uh..."

"Come here, Gene." Juliet smiled and pulled Eugene in for a hug. "I have so much to tell you. But there's yet another obstacle preventing me from doing that."

"You think I'd want you to go in there without me?" Eugene held her tight, taking in the fragrance of her skin. "I may not be an assassin, but I can hold my own."

"Ha. I bet I can still kick your ass." Juliet giggled and clenched him tighter.

"Yeah, but it would be a bit more fun this time." Eugene pressed his face into her neck, and pulled her as close to him as possible. This was what he'd wanted for years, and he couldn't imagine not having it again.

****

Somewhere Outside of North Bend, Nebraska

The somber snowy cornfields of Nebraska sat untarnished and silent for a moment before the caravan of government vehicles, overseen by two helicopters, burrowed their way through the thick of it. Beside the two helicopters, the caravan contained a massive bus style command center, followed by ten SUVs and a few Humvee like vehicles containing an eighty-five-person invading force. Each were equipped with body cameras, an earpiece to command, an assault rifle and handgun, thermal grenades, flares, and enough ammunition to last the day.

"All right, here's the deal, folks. We've located a few emergency hatch exits as well as a main bunker entrance. Once on site, we will establish a command unit, and wait for Miss Cubro to infiltrate the bunker. Then team one will advance on the main entrance, and teams two and three will advance on the hatches. Be prepared to witness things you've never seen before. We just got word from Seattle that Jessica Davis was killed after she mutated into a creature of some kind with extraordinary strength and agility. I expect we might find something like that down below. Either way, the likelihood that they don't know we're coming is slim. So be sharp, and be ready."

Riley, Eugene, and Juliet met Director Locke and a few other tech agents in the Command Unit. The unit was covered with monitors, constantly switching back from the different body cameras of the various teams. Riley and Eugene were dressed in standard tactical gear, while Juliet had her own skin-tight textured suit made of a highly advanced bullet-resistant fabric, and accented with armor enhanced pads on each of her joints.

"All right. Teams are in place. I want Agent Riley to join team two, and Mr. Pierce can join team three. You're up, Miss Cubro. We'll give you a few minutes head start." Director Locke handed Juliet a body cam and headgear set. "I'll need you to wear these so we can stay in contact and watch your progress."

"I don't need it. I just need to give you access to my frequency." Locke had a confused look on his face as Juliet relieved one of the tech agents and began running an access program on the computer. Within moments, the screen changed to reflect what Juliet saw. "Now you see what I see. I've tapped into your network as well, so I'll hear your troop-wide commands, or you can contact me directly."

"Well you're just full of tricks." Director Locke leaned down to look at Juliet's pupils, as his image zoomed in on the computer screen.

"Can you take any weapons?" Eugene leaned against the side of the command unit, checking his sidearm.

"The implant that allows me to transport is programmed to recognize my body mass. It's adjustable, so I'm able to bring some basic things like my knives. I'll pick up something more substantial when I get inside." Stepping outside, Juliet secured a handful of daggers to her belt, as well as two thin swords, crisscrossing over her back. She threw herself at Eugene, hugging him tightly.

"Be careful, please." Eugene held her tight. "We've still got a lot to talk about, when this is all over."

"I know." Juliet kissed his cheek and then stepped back. "You be careful, too. I'll see you on the other side."

Juliet lifted her sleeve and touched the anchor tattoo on her right forearm. As she felt implant activate, she began to bounce on her feet a bit, daggers in hand, preparing herself for the jump. Between her hired contracts, Juliet had found time to hunt down the few people she knew to have involvement with M.O.R.S., but nothing to this level. She was ready. She was eager. As the space around her blurred into light, Juliet tightened her grip on the daggers and prepared herself for anything. Completing the jump, Juliet found herself on a teleportation pad in a row of large, open-faced vertical cylinders in what appeared to be a locker room.

As her eyes adjusted, though, she suddenly saw what filled the room in front of her. She felt her sense of determination change to utter shock, and then to defeat in the matter of a second. In the center of the room were a group of barrels, marked flammable, laced with wires that connected to several sticks of dynamite, all hooked into a digital timer that had two seconds left on it. Juliet sighed, and looked away.

****

"Oh, God, no…" Riley, Locke, and Eugene watched from the monitors as the seconds ran out on the time.

"No, no, no! Juliet!" Eugene watched as the barrels exploded, obliterating the room and cutting the feed from Juliet's frequency. Eugene dropped to the floor. Riley grabbed him and pulled him back to his feet.

"I'm sorry, Eugene, but this isn't the time for grief. We've got to get to our teams, now!"

Eugene nodded and gripped his rifle as the two exited the unit and made their separate ways across the snowy cornfields toward their teams.

"All teams, this is Director Locke. We have a go for breach. Sound off and get in there." Locke switched the monitors to show the body cams of the team leaders.

"We're moving in. Team One is on the move, Agent Feregrino out."

"Team Two is breaching the hatch. Agent Gambino out!"

"Team Three is beginning its descent down the second hatch. Agent Everly out!"

Team One neared the blast doors of the main entrance. The underside of a large hill had been carved out on the west side to make room for two large blast doors, wide enough to fit two Humvees through, side by side. The team split up to plant charges on the four massive hinges on the corners of the two doors. They packed C4 into the middle, running from the top to the bottom of the doors. The team took cover and pressed the detonator. A colossal **BOOM** shook the hillside as the doors fell to the ground. While they may have been built fifty years ago to withstand a nuclear blast, a few modern demolition charges placed at specific points could bring it down.

As all teams made their way inside the facility, they each found the same thing—nothing. There was no army waiting to engage them, no creatures dragging them off into the shadows, just empty and quiet hallways with the lights on. As Eugene's team pushed forward, they could smell smoke in the air, and Eugene made his way down a side hall to find that half of it had been burned to a crisp. Weapon at his side, Eugene stood in front of a room on fire, its doors blown off their hinges, stuck in the wall behind him. Eugene could feel his skin flare with the heat as he stared into the flames. Somewhere, in the heat, was his Juliet—what was left of her.

Agent Riley's team caught up with team one as both of their hallways met in a large lobby with a huge map of the world engraved into the wall. There was a bank of computers beneath it.

M.O.R.S. INITIATIVE was engraved on top of the map, but someone had written something over the top of the display in bold, dripping red paint: **WE ARE EVERYWHERE.**

"There's no one here, Director. It's like they knew we were coming and cleared out," Riley spoke into her headset as one of the agents hooked up a device to one of the computers in an attempt to hack it. Suddenly a crackling noise filled the room as the loud speakers on the walls above them came on.

"Hello, Agent Harper and friends! Welcome to our little home!"

Riley's men each raised their weapons and took positions at each hallway opening.

"I would have thrown a welcome party for you, but….well everyone had to leave. Don't worry, though, I've left some surprises for you. I think I might even stick around for a while, and watch you all die."

Eugene heard the voice as he continued to stare into the flames, his hand tightening around the grip of his rifle.

"And to you, Mr. Pierce, don't worry about your little science experiment of a friend. I'm sure she didn't feel too much of the skin melting off her bones."

"All teams converge on my location. We know there are levels beneath us. We need to go in as one." Riley's voice sounded across the com links.

Eugene took one last look into the fire, his now almost beginning to singe as he starred into the heat.

"Eugene. Do you copy?"

"On my way." Eugene turned away from the flame and jogged down the hall to meet back up with his group.

****

Together as one massive team, the agents followed Riley through a door at the end of the corridor that led to a glass stairwell going down five floors. The stairwell was mounted on a wall next to a giant, five-story mural of what appeared to be planets and stars. Engraved in huge letters were four simple words: ***TO RULE AND REIGN***.

The team kept moving down another corridor towards an unmarked set of double doors. With agents covering her on either side, Riley pushed open the doors to reveal a massive dark room. She couldn't see anything, but she heard the echo of the doors, and felt the breeze, as if she was walking into a large auditorium or gymnasium. Near the door was a large lever. Knowing their flashlights would not provide accurate coverage, Riley grabbed the lever and shoved it down, hoping it would turn on some lights. One by one, large lights began to slowly illuminate on the ceiling five stories overhead, revealing an enormous room. Another mural on the wall showed several faceless figures, standing at least forty feet high, next to another engraved phrase: ***THE NEW YOU!***

The space, large enough to fill at least three football fields, was mostly bare. The only exception was a laboratory set up in the middle of the room. The team spread out across the area, as Riley and Eugene led a unit towards the open lab. Large tanks of water stood next to each other, each containing deformed bodies of men and women. Some bodies had large swelling bumps all over, others appeared to be inside out with their organs visible on the outside, and others had massive bones protruding from the inside. The lab had several operating tables, equipment to process bloodwork, and enough cameras to film it all.

"What the hell is this?" Before Riley could get a second look, however, the room went black as the lights above shut off. Agents kicked on their flashlights, but they paled in comparison to the massive dark space. The voice came over the loud speakers again.

"I apologize for the inconvenience, but how do you expect me to surprise you with all the lights on?"

"Pop flares if you have them!" Riley popped the top of her flare and threw it to the ground at the far side of the lab area. The flashlights covered half of the space, while agents attempted to throw their flares far enough to cover the other half. As Riley returned her eyes to the large tanks, she heard something in the distance.

Splat! Splat! Splat! Splat!

The sounds were getting louder, as they multiplied from the far side of the room, as if several people were running barefoot across the open floor. Riley raised her weapon and aimed towards the dark until, without warning, the noises stopped.

"Does anyone see anything?"

"Something's out there."

"Someone get these lights back on!"

"I can't see shit!"

"Wait, there! What is that?" An agent near Riley pointed toward the dark. Two blue balls of light seemed to levitate in the darkness. "Are those.....eyes?"

As if to answer the agent, the pair of blue lights came closer and began to rise about twelve feet off the ground. Riley popped another flare and threw it toward the lights. It landed on the hard floor and rolled to a stop. Suddenly a large scaly foot with talons stepped on top of the flare. Into the light stepped a humongous beast, at least twelve feet high and as wide as a minivan. The creature appear to be humanoid, as it stood on two legs and had the same, if not exaggerated, body structure of a human. It had no skin, but just exposed bone, muscles, and dark red veiny tendons running across its frame. Its forearms appeared to be huge masses of bone from the elbow down to the claws. Two rows of jagged, hideous fangs made their way up and down the creatures jaw beneath two glowing holes where the eyes would be. The creature cocked its head and roared ferociously as several other sets of glowing lights appeared in the distance behind it, belonging to other creatures of the same hideous appearance but varying in shapes and sizes; tall and skinny, short and stout.

"Open fire! Do it!" Riley raised her assault rifle, set it to full auto, and pulled back the trigger. The creature shrieked and growled as bullets dug into its mass. It dropped down to four legs and seemed to gallop toward the closest cluster of agents. It swung its arm against two agents, sending them flying to the dark, while it dug its claws through the chest of another agent. When it ripped its claws out, the agent fell to pieces, like pulled pork, onto the floor.

Riley found cover behind one of the water tanks and scanned the area for Eugene. Gunfire lit the massive room sporadically as Riley watched some creatures gallop toward their victims, while others climbed the walls and dove down upon their prey. Some sprinted at incredible speed on two legs as they ran their claws through crowds of agents, dismembering anything they came across.

****

Samuel Stoke watched the chaos from his office window, overlooking the entire space. He smiled as he returned to his desk and grabbed his phone. Dialing the number one speed dial, he poured himself a final glass from his favorite bottle of Polish scotch, Dark Whisky. The phone rang once or twice before it was picked up.

"The enemy is being obliterated as we speak," he said. "My team has already evacuated, and I'm about ready to leave myself."

"Good work, Samuel." The female voice on the other end sounded pleased. "Be sure there's nothing left for anyone to recover. Feel free to lay low once you've evacuated, while we determine where next to set you up."

"Thank you, madam. I will." Samuel hung up the phone and took the last gulp of scotch before sitting down at his desk and opening a program on his computer. "This place will be nothing but a hole in the ground, soon enough."

****

The chaos was unrelenting, as screams and shouting filled the spaces between gunfire and blood-curdling shrieks from the creatures. Bullets were useless against the creatures as they barely slowed down any attack.

An agent near Riley was tackled to the floor by a skinny-framed monster crouched over him. Riley loaded another magazine into her rifle as she stood up and sprayed the creature with several rounds of ammunition. As the creature turned toward Riley, the agent's shredded throat in its teeth, Riley aimed for its head and pulled the trigger. Several bullets dug into the creature's skull before it finally went down.

Riley heard someone yelled, and turned her head to see Eugene flying through the air into one of the tanks. The tank shattered and sent Eugene to the floor in waves of water and glass.

****

As Eugene groaned in pain, pulling a piece of glass out of his forehead, he looked up to see one of the larger creatures walking towards him. He searched for his rifle, but it was no longer by his side. Another agent stepped in front of Eugene and fired upon the beast. The beast's two claws came down upon the agent in a crisscrossing stroke. The agent's body was separated in three places as his hand gripped his weapon and continued to fire, aimlessly into the dark, before bleeding to death in a heap on the floor. The creature looked down at the body, and then looked back to Eugene.

"Ah, damn." Eugene struggled to get to his feet but kept slipping in the water. "Any help here? Please!"

Riley ran towards him, firing her rifle at the creature, but it didn't seem distracted at all. Within moments the creature loomed over him, roaring at an ear-shattering decibel.

Suddenly a figure ran in front of Eugene, slashing across the open space with a sword in each hand. One blade slashed through the beast's leg, just under the knee, with one clean stroke. The beast shrieked in pain as it stumbled to the floor in front of Eugene. Eugene crawled backwards as quickly as he could, as he watched the figure jump into the air behind the creature and thrust the two swords deep into its back. Rolling off the creature, the figure grabbed a handful of unused flares of the body of a fallen agent, and ran towards the monster's good leg. Sliding under the creature, the figure fired several rounds into the beast's thigh, creating a large enough gash to stick the bundle of flares in.

"Get clear!"

The figure dove under a table and fired at the bundle of flares. The bundle exploded inside the beast's thigh, burning its way straight through until the detached leg fell to the floor and the beast as well. As the creature howled in pain and struggled to crawl away, the figure walked onto its back, pulled out the two swords and then brought them down, each piercing one of the monster's eye sockets. As the beast shrieked a final time before its head hit the floor, the figure turned toward Eugene.

"Juliet! But how?" Eugene was as excited as he was shocked to see her. He felt a swell of emotions with him, as he tried to make out her face in the dark.

Juliet walked towards him in the dark.

"Like I said, Eugene, there are still things I haven't told you." Juliet stepped into the light to reveal that half of her face has been burned away, leaving a glossed over white eyeball, and nothing but charred ligaments and bone on the right side of her face. "But we don't have time for that now. Samuel Stoke is still here, and we have to get to him. There's an elevator this way!"

****

"All agents on me!" Riley pulled Eugene to his feet and sprinted after Juliet All around them, agents fought to stay alive. A handful of agents nearby joined the group as they ran for the elevator. One of the faster creatures sprinted out of the shadows and tackled one of the agents to the ground. Another creature ran between the group and the elevator, but Juliet threw two daggers into its chest before slicing off its head with her sword.

The group crowded into the elevator and quickly trained their firearms toward the screams and gunfire until the doors were closed. The elevator rose toward Stoke's penthouse suite and seemed to take forever to get there. No one said a word, as they each struggled to catch their breath and tried to hold onto the brief sense of security while locked in the elevator. The doors opened to a large room with an office space on one side and a bar on the other. In the middle, surrounded by guards, sat a smiling Samuel Stoke. The handful of men around him, dressed in the same faceless black tactical gear that Riley had seen at Summerhill, had their weapons raised and trained on Riley's group.

"Don't move, Stoke!" Riley stood in front of her group as they fanned out behind her.

"I wouldn't dream of it, Agent Harper. Although you aren't necessarily in any position to be making demands." Stoke sat in a lounge chair, a martini cocktail in hand.

"Where's Peter?" Riley stepped closer, pointing her gun at Samuel's face. "Tell me, dammit!"

"Oh, you mean your little policeman?" Stoke pointed a remote toward a wall full of flat screen monitors. Each one suddenly brought a video feed, shot from different angles, of Peter being dragged into a room and strapped down to a chair. Peter was shouting and trying to get free, but it was no use. Several doctors surrounded him, each holding different size needles that they stuck into various points on his body; between his fingers, his neck, his forearms and shoulders, under his knees and into his calves. Another doctor took a small drill and began making a hole in the side of Peter's head. His screams filled the room as Riley watched in horror. Whatever they had injected into him appear force Peter to remain conscious as the small drill bit was removed from his skull. A needle was inserted into the hole as Peter cried out in pain, tears streaming down his face to mix with the blood flowing out of his ears, nose, and mouth.

"Let's just say he was unable to make it here, Agent Harper." Stoke smirked a nasty smile as he swish his drink in the glass.

"You sick son of a bitch!" Riley stepped another foot forward.

"Stand down, Harper! We need him alive," Riley heard Director Locke screaming through her earpiece.

"If it helps, your little friend endured more than eight hours of this without breaking. We had to keep reviving him of course, as we treated him to so many forms of torture. Just for kicks and giggles." Samuel removed the toothpick from his cocktail and ate the attached green olive. He appear to notice the horrified look on Eugene's face and smiled. "Don't look so shocked, Mr. Pierce. This is child's play compared to the things your mother used to do.

"And you, Juliet, how I've missed you. No matter how much of a thorn in our side you've become, there will always be a special place in my heart for you. You are such a sight for sore eyes."

Juliet pulled a dagger from her belt and hissed at Stoke.

"I hope one day to hear how you acquired that name, Juliet," Stoke continued. "Did you give it to yourself? Did someone else give it to you? It certainly suits you better than the number we had assigned to you. I'm sure you remember all of our most violently intimate times together in Sarajevo. Of course, I would probably prefer that over what your agents are going through right now."

Stoke clicked the remote again to show a variety of cameras switching back and forth from one horrific scene to another. Agents were being slaughtered all over the facility, as they attempted to find shelter from the creatures. One screen showed a creature ripping out an agent's throat, while another showed two beasts ripping an agent limb from limb. The screens were filled with footage of men and women dying in the most horrifically gruesome ways. Soon the cameras simply panned over hallways of dismembered bodies, as the creatures fled to search for other lively victims.

"I'd love to stay and cherish these moments with you further," Stoke said, "but my men and I have a helicopter to catch."

A hidden door on the far side of the room opened as Stoke and his men eased their way toward the door. Riley, Juliet, and Eugene followed alongside the other agents, keeping their weapons trained on their individual targets.

Riley stood in awe as she stepped through the door into the belly of a former missile silo. At one point, this space had been occupied by a weapon of mass destruction, ready to wreak havoc on the poor soul that provoked the United States. Now, the silo had been retrofitted, widened and carved out, to serve as a makeshift vertical hanger just large enough for a military grade helicopter.

"Don't worry, guys, I'm not leaving you to the fate of those creatures. While you won't be able to follow me out of this silo, you won't need to test your fate in the facility either. This whole place is rigged to blow in a matter of minutes." Samuel stepped inside the helicopter as one of his men took control of one of the two mounted machine guns. Samuel looked down at his watch and smiled. "Nineteen minutes and thirty-five seconds to be exact! Take care, my friends!"

Samuel closed the helicopter door and it lifted off the ground, as Riley clicked a stopwatch function on her watch. The agents around Riley opened fire upon the bird, but their bullets were wasted. Riley looked up to see the bay doors open about three hundred feet above them. As the helicopter rose toward the opening, Riley called out to Director Locke on her headset.

"Stoke's escaping! He's got a knock-off Apache helicopter and he's coming your way!"

****

"We're on it, Agent Harper." Director Locke exited the command unit to a house-size hole open in the ground not fifty feet from him. Locke's two helicopters surrounded the hole, waiting for Samuel's ride to appear. As it emerged from the ground, Locke spoke into his headset, which was connected to a massive loudspeaker attached to one of his birds in the sky.

"Samuel Stoke, you are under arrest. Land your aircraft or you will be met with force!"

Stoke's helicopter hovered in the air for a second, as if deciding what to do. When it continued its ascent into the sky, Locke gave the signal for his birds to open fire. Stoke's helicopter banked to the left to avoid the brunt of one line of fire, while taking hits from the second chopper. The armor plating protected Stoke's bird from major damage as it fired off a few missiles in response. One of Locke's helicopters exploded on impact with a missile, while the other took a hit on its back rotor and went spiraling toward the ground. The enemy helicopter's aerial gun then opened fire on the parked caravan of military vehicles. Locke took cover for the brief moment of fire until Stoke's helicopter adjusted course and flew off into the west.

"Agent Harper! Stoke got away. What's your status?" Locke returned to the command unit and searched for a body cam that had Riley in its sights.

"We've got about sixteen minutes before this place goes up in flames. There's no way to exit through the silo, and there isn't enough time to make our way back through the structure. Can you send one of your birds down to pick us up?"

Locke sighed and lowered his head in defeat. "Both choppers are down, and we have no other way of reaching through the silo opening." Locke switched views until it focused on Juliet. "What about you, Miss Cubro? Any options?"

"I can only think of one, but we're running short on time. In my duffle bag is a large rectangular slab, about the side of two laptops. I need you take it outside and hook it up to the generator you have powering your command unit. If we can get it up and running in time, I might be able to get some of these people out."

Director Locke ran out of the command unit and to the SUV that Juliet had ridden in earlier. Grabbing the large duffel bag from the trunk, Locke doubled back toward the command unit. Two of his men were already ripping off a panel to the generator as Lock pulled the heavy metal slab from the duffle and dropped it on the ground. The slab had a slot in its side, designed to fit an industrial power distribution cable.

One of Locke's agents flipped a switch to shut down the generator as the other pulled free the thick power cable. Locke inserted it into the slab, and his agent flipped the generator on again. Locke stepped back as the slab of metal came alive as flaps began to unfold from the slide, multiplying it into a large space. The separate flaps then began to twist together until they formed a circle just wide enough for two people to stand on.

"The unit is ready, Miss Cubro. Are you?"

****

Juliet desperately fiddled with the computer screen on her forearm as she tried to adjust her implant's settings to account for the additional weight of carrying someone. Riley, Eugene, and the rest of the agents had returned to the lounge room to cover the silo.

A few more agents had made their way up the elevator, but there didn't seem to be any left. The creatures in the massive room beneath the lounge seemed to take notice of the survivors as they began climbing the walls towards the lounge's windows.

"We're running out of time Juliet," Riley called as she helped her men push furniture toward the windows to try to secure them for as long as they could. "Thirteen minutes!"

"I've got it, but I'll only be able to take one of you at a time. Gene, get over here now!"

Eugene ran to Juliet and wrapped his arm around her as she pressed the anchor tattoo on her forearm. They disappear in a ball of light, as the first creature reached the windows and began pounding against the reinforced glass. Juliet and Eugene reappeared on the portable receiver unit next to Locke's command center as they crashed to the ground.

"Yes! It worked!"

Locke looked at Juliet, relieved, but then frowned in confusion. "How are you going to get back down there if there isn't another unit to receive you?"

Juliet gave him a look of despair as she stood and took off sprinting off across the snow toward the silo's opening in the ground. Running as fast as she could, Juliet leap out into the open air above the hole, and prepared for the fall.

****

Riley turned around to see Juliet falling the three hundred or so feet before landing on the floor of the silo in a deafening *BOOM*. Juliet stumbled to her feet and ran towards the closet agent. Tackling him to the ground, Juliet pressed the anchor tattoo, and the two of them disappeared.

Riley returned her focus toward the cracks that began to form across the lounge windows. Five of the skinny framed monster were now trying to break the glass. Riley knew this fight would be over in seconds if she couldn't find some way to buy Juliet more time. Darting over to the bar, Riley began grabbing bottles off the shelves. Stuffing hand towels down the necks of each hard liquor bottle she could find, she slid them one by one toward the remaining agents. Another *BOOM* sounded as Juliet returned and grabbed another agent.

Riley was now left with eight other agents as the each popped flares and stood with their liquor bottles. Riley took a swig of scotch before stuffing a torn piece of her shirt down the bottle and rejoining formation with her men. Her watch said that they had about nine minutes left before the facility exploded, but she didn't have time to think about that. The real threat was right in front of them as a hole finally began to form in the glass.

"Do it!"

Riley lit her bottle's rag with a flare and threw it toward the couch and cushioned chairs lined up against the glass. The bottle exploded, along with the others, and a great fire began to form between Riley's men and the glass. Another *BOOM* came behind them as Juliet stumbled in the room. She was clearly weakened, but she continued on as she grabbed another agent and disappeared in a flash.

"Hurry, Juliet!"

The first creature dug its way through the glass and fell into the flames. The agents opened fire as the beast wailed in sheer pain. Another hole opened in the glass and two more monsters crawled through. Riley and her men began to back away toward the hangar door as they continued to fire upon the creatures. Riley grabbed a grenade from her belt and chucked it towards the bar as she joined her fellow agents in the silo. Three more creatures burst through the glass and into the room just before the grenade exploded and filled the room with flame. Riley quickly loaded her last magazine into her sidearm, as she took a defensive firing position with her men at the far side of the silo.

A twelve-foot beast emerged from the lounge, covered in flame, and stumbled into the silo. Hopping over its back were two more smaller monsters, each shrieking as they tried to fan off the flames from their bodies. Riley opened fire with the rest of her men as the creatures galloped for them. The agents on either side of her were slammed against the silo wall as the creatures tore into them. The large monster hovered above Riley and roared as she emptied the remainder of her magazine into its chest and face. Suddenly a loud **BOOM** sounded behind the creature, as Juliet crashed into the silo's floor. The creature turned and advanced toward Juliet, but she quickly dove between its legs and ran for Riley. Grabbing onto each other, Juliet pressed her fingers against her tattoo and closed her eyes. Riley watched as the creatures dove for them, but then a bright light flashed and suddenly she was falling to the snow-covered ground at Locke's feet.

"Is there anyone left?" Locke carried one of his men toward a nearby Humvee.

"None that can be saved. We need to get out of here now!" Juliet helped up Riley as they sprinted toward a second Humvee with Eugene behind the wheel.

With everyone on board, the two vehicles accelerated down the road as fast as they could. Riley stuck her head out of the window and peered back toward the silo's opening in the field. To her horror, Riley saw a multitude of creatures reach the surface. The creatures roared and shrieked as they began to gallop across the snow.

Riley's watch beeped.

A deep resounding rumble suddenly shook the ground as a loud blast bellowed from beneath the surface. Before the creatures could reach a safe distance from the silo, the ground around them suddenly shot up into the sky as a huge wall of flame rose from the earth. The blast wave shook the Humvees as they tackled the terrain at top speed. When they reached a half mile distance, the Humvees pulled over and the group dismounted to watch as a humongous mushroom cloud formed in the sky. The site was glorious and disturbing all at the same time. If the M.O.R.S. Initiative could amass this much destruction simply to cover their tracks, Riley wondered just how much damage they could inflict upon the world.

14 HATS OFF AND HELLO

Thompson Toys, Somewhere in Vermont

Three days later, Riley sat in her chair at the secret base, next to Juliet and Eugene, opposite Director Locke as he reviewed her report of the Nebraska incident. In one hour, Riley and Locke were due to board their flight to Virginia, for a meeting at the Central Intelligence Agency headquarters . Also due at the meeting were hand-picked heads of state, foreign and domestic intelligence agencies, and other invited parties. Riley and Locke would inform them all of the situation with M.O.R.S. Locke seemed pleased with Riley's account of the events and put down the report.

"You folks look terrible. Except for you, Juliet. Somehow you look brand new."

Riley was nursing a few wounds on her face, neck and arms. Eugene has a bandage around his forehead covering his head wound. Juliet, however, had no visible signs of physical damage. "

"While the facility was obliterated beyond any possible degree of recovery," Locke went on, "the mission was not a failure. The explosion rid us of the daunting task of addressing Samuel Stoke's creature infestation. We were able to wirelessly upload a few gigs of data recovered from our attempt to hack their computers. We also have recovered some interesting data recorded from the body cam footage of our agents on site. It's not much, but we will do what we can to piece it all together to figure out our next move.

"So far, this is what we've gathered. We've confirmed Juliet's suspicions that M.O.R.S. is actually an acronym for its four founders. We know that 'S' stands for Stoke, and 'R' stands for Reynolds. As they're both big names in very specific industries, human genetics and pharmaceuticals, we have a running theory that the other two names will belong to heads of other vital industries. We found enough to confirm our other theories on the branches of the organization."

The monitor behind Locke flicked on to display a flow chart with House of M.O.R.S. at the top.

"The House of M.O.R.S. reigns supreme over three smaller divisions—the M.O.R.S. Initiative, the Church of MORS, and the Hand of M.O.R.S. This confirmation will help us to funnel our efforts into finding specific targets that would match the needs of these divisions.

"That's enough of the lesson for now. Mr. Pierce, Miss Cubro, you are dismissed." Eugene and Juliet both nodded and left the room.

Riley remained in her seat, head lowered, facing the floor. After all that she had done, she had failed to find Peter, and their mission had delivered the most minimal of fruits.

"I know you've been through a lot, Riley. The loss of a partner is never easy. So I'd understand if you need a break. But if you don't, I have a mission for you."

Riley raised her head, suddenly sharp with attention.

"Obviously our intel is time sensitive, so you won't have long to decide. Your mission would begin immediately after our meeting this afternoon."

"I'm ready, sir." Riley sat up, full of adrenaline, as if someone had breathed new life into her. "More than ready."

****

Eugene and Juliet walked down the hallway toward the exit. While Eugene had agreed to stay on as an official member of the unit, Juliet had preferred to remain as a consultant; she had enough on her plate and didn't want to be under the government's thumb any more than she needed to be.

Juliet reached out and grabbed Eugene's hand, but he wasn't quick to hold hers in return. When they reached the warehouse room full of Thompson Teddy Bears, Eugene stopped and turned toward Juliet.

"So when are you going to tell me the whole story?" He leaned back against a shelf and kept a short distance from Juliet.

"I think you know the highlights of it, Gene." Juliet shrugged and smiled as Eugene tried to mask the clear discomfort on his face. "I wasn't just experimented on in Sarajevo. I was created there, and that freaks you out. Doesn't it?"

"I guess." Eugene lowered his head.

Juliet stepped forward and wrapped her arms around him. He hugged her back as they both dug their heads into each other. "I still love you, Juliet."

"I know." Juliet hugged him as tight as she could.

"But…"

"I know." Juliet didn't need to hear him say the words. It was clear that he was struggling with her being less of a human and more of a manufactured weapon. She wasn't a robot, but the fact that her existence had been designed and programmed since birth was just as much of a departure.

****

The two broke their hug, and Eugene escorted Juliet out of the warehouse. Standing in the morning sun, he took in her beauty for one last time. She was every bit as beautiful as the first day he had seen her. Her eyes were just as piercing, her smile just as enticing, and her general presence lifted his spirit. He couldn't help but look at her differently, though, now knowing how different from him she really way.

"I'll miss you." Eugene wanted to say more, but he couldn't find the words.

"I'll be around." Juliet smiled back at him, but as she pressed the anchor tattoo on her arm, her smile faded. She was hurt, and Eugene knew it. As Juliet disappeared in front of him, Eugene stood there for a moment and looked at the slab of concrete where she had stood. He knew it wasn't right. He knew Juliet had wanted more. He couldn't deny his feelings, but he couldn't deny his hesitations either. Sighing, Eugene tucked his hands into his pocks and turned to take stroll between the abandoned warehouses.

****

Virginia

When Riley and Director Locke arrived at CIA headquarters, ,she couldn't help but feel a bit nostalgic. She missed being an FBI agent. Murder, kidnapping, drug cases were so much simpler than her reality now. While she was content to be a part of something bigger, something that mattered, she couldn't help but feel disconnected from normal life.

Once she and Director Locke made it through the metal detectors and cleared the front desk, Riley followed him up the escalators to the second floor.

Suddenly she heard a commotion in the lobby behind her and turned around to see what was going on.

"Riley! Riley Harper! Wait!"

Riley turned to see Peter Drake calling out her name while he tried to force his way past the visitor line. The metal detectors went off as he bolted through them and into the center of the lobby. Guards came from every direction to converge on Peter as he dropped to his knees and interlaced his fingers behind his head.

"Wait! Back off that man! Give him some space," Riley cried out as she made her way back down the escalators. The guards formed a perimeter around Peter, as others escorted the visitors out the front door; clearing the area.

"Peter! You're alive!" Riley attempted to run toward Peter, but Locke grabbed her by the arm and held her back.

Peter saw this, and his smile immediately disappeared. As he stood up, Riley noticed that he'd lost at least twenty pounds, and now appeared to be a frail shadow of what he used to be. He stood there in dirty jeans and a t-shirt, looking at Riley with a sense of dread on his face.

"For now, Riley. Only for now. The House of M.O.R.S. kept me alive only to deliver you a message. They wanted to tip their hats off to you, to congratulate you on your small victory in Nebraska. The facility was nothing but a pawn on their chessboard."

He stepped toward Riley as he spoke, but the guards shouted for him to stop as they trained their side arms on him.

Peter sighed and stopped. "They wanted to remain in the shadows for a while longer, but now is as good a time as any to introduce themselves. The sent me here to formally say hello, and to wish you good luck in stopping them from completing their goals."

"What goals would those be, Officer Drake?" Locke stepped forward.

Riley only then noticed that Peter's arm was shaking. Peter grabbed it and tried to settle the nerve, but it was no use. He looked up at Director Locke in tears as he desperately tried to hold back from massive pain.

"They want to destroy the world! They want to force us into the next stage of evolution. Agh!"

Peter dropped to the floor. Blood dripped from his nose. He began to cough until he spit up stream of blood and mucus. A quarantine alarm sounded as all exits were suddenly blocked by metal doors.

"Everybody stay back! We don't know what he has," one of the guards shouted, but Riley knew exactly what was going on. Peter looked up from the floor, blood now draining from his eyes.

Riley stepped toward him through the perimeter of guards, shoving off their attempts to hold her back.

"I'm so sorry, Riley! I tried, but I couldn't get back to you. You're the only thing that's kept me alive till now, but I can't go on any farther."

"I know, Peter." Riley knelt down beside him and caressed his face as Peter's teeth began to fall out one by one, and the bones of his spine cracked, then burst through his skin and shirt.

"Please! Please, Riley. You have to do it now, or I'll kill everyone in this room! Please," Peter begged with profound despair in his eyes. He continued to cough up more blood onto the floor. Riley stepped back and pulled out her sidearm.

"I'm sorry, Peter. I'll make them pay for this." Riley took off the safety and aimed her gun at Peter as a tear escaped down her cheek.

Peter raised his eyebrows as he pleaded for the end, offering one last human expression before rabid anger appeared on his face and he growled and hissed.

Riley pulled the trigger and fired a bullet straight into Peter's forehead. Peter fell back onto the floor and exhaled. She walked over to his body and stared down at his warped face. She fired her gun again, and again, and again, until she emptied her entire magazine into his body.

"I swear it, Peter."

.

EPILOGUE

Somewhere in Louisiana

Riley walked down the highway with her arm extended, holding her thumb up to any driver that drove past. Her hair was cut short to a pixie style, and dyed dark brown. She wore a hoodie and a dirty pair of jeans, with a backpack of snacks and change of clothes, hanging from her shoulder.

She was tired and hungry, and she had been on the road for a few days now, following the highway south towards Texas. The sun had only just set, but the air was already chilly, as Riley tucked her free hand into her hoodie. The full moon glowed overhead as Riley tried to keep her strength and continue walking. A large semi-truck and trailer pulled over behind her, and Riley turned around to face its blinding headlights. The driver exited the truck and walked over to meet her.

Riley sighed and almost doubled over in exhaustion as she finally let her arm fall to her side.

"Are you all right? What's your name, miss?"

"Alissa Lynn," Riley croaked. They were the first words she'd spoken in days. She was parched, and her throat was beyond sore from inhaling all the dust kicked up from the road.

"That's a pretty name." The overweight truck drive attempted to suck in his gut as he approached her. He had a thick beard and a Coor's Light truck hat to match his blue plaid long-sleeved shirt. "Where ya heading, Alissa?"

"Nowhere, really." Riley shrugged and looked up at the man from beneath her hoodie. The driver smiled and held out a bottle of water. Riley grabbed the bottle quickly and chugged as much as she could.

"Well, there isn't a homeless shelter anywhere nearby, but I know of a big tent revival up the way. If you wanna come with me, I can get ya there in time for the supper and sermon."

Riley wiped her face and smiled back at the truck driver. She followed him back to the truck and

THE FIERCE ARE FADING

climbed into the passenger seat. As the driver eased the rig back onto the road, he passed her a blanket.

"Now you just get some rest and I'll let you know when we get there."

Riley balled up under the blanket as she peered out the window at the open sky of stars. She had waited for this moment for days, knowing it would eventually come, but aching to quit with every passing moment. Now that she was able to rest, her mind wondered back to the last time she saw Director Locke. His words rang true inside her brain.

"The facility left us with more questions than answers, Agent Harper. Whatever Stoke was injecting into those people, it still evades our top scientists. There are theories, outlandish ones, but I'm making the time to consider them. Right now, the only actionable intel we have is on the cult branch down in Panama.

"You're going to need to get down there, and imbed yourself amongst the weak and hopeless. You can't have fun, and I can't give you a radio, or a wire, or any form of communication. You'll need to go in naked. If they suspect you, they'll kill you.

"You'll need to change your appearance, Riley. Change your name, too. You're in their sights now, and while I'd rather send a newer agent on this mission, I knew

your stubbornness would not allow anyone else to go but you. We've gathered some information about pickup points along the Bible belt. You'll need to start there."

The truck driver dropped Riley off beside an open field with a large circus tent erected in the middle. Riley stumbled across the grass as she neared the entrance. She clung onto the blanket that the driver had given her as she locked eyes with one of the ushers in front of the tent. The usher welcomed her with open arms, gave her a bowl of soup and a piece of bread, and escorted her into the tent to find a seat in front of a massive stage. The tent was full of a variety of different people; homeless people, families, business men and women in worn suits, church going elder folks, and lost and lonely teenagers. A man with silver hair mounted the stage and addressed the crowd.

"Welcome, strangers! I can see you've all been called here for a purpose. You may not know what you believe, but deep down you know that there is a need within you; a burning need for change! And I'm here to tell you how we're going to make that change happen!" The crowd cheered and clapped, but Riley crossed her arms and peered up at the man. "This world has come to a halt, ladies and gentlemen. It's been worn down with all its laziness and wickedness.

"They want you to pay for the right to live on this earth. Electricity bills, house loans, gas for your vehicles, data for your cell phones, Christmas presents for your relatives, roses for your loved ones, taxes for your water. There's never an end to it. The evils of society have burrowed their way into our lives, and we need an escape. I'm here to tell you that there is a high power that calls upon each of us to fix this earth; to cleanse it of these evils, and bring it back to the Eden it was intended to be. He calls upon all of us. On you, and you, and you!

"Now the Romans called it MORS, but we know it as the wrath of God. It is our duty to carry out his wrath upon the world, and bring it to justice once more. But before we can do that, we have to reunite with our former selves; our kinder, more peaceful, pure selves. I'm sorry, ladies and gentlemen, but you will never find that side of yourself where you are now, surrounded by the evils of this world.

"So I invite you to come away with me. There is a place out there, a place of solitude and righteousness. It is the closest thing we can find to Eden, and it serves as the shelter where we can cleanse ourselves of the vile we've got stuck under our skin."

Riley looked around to see ushers making their way down the aisles, passing large plates back and forth.

"There are gentlemen making the rounds throughout this tent. I ask that you give up your petty belongings and join me. You don't need your phones, your credit cards, your debt or personal ties where we're going.

"Now, you came here because you're lost. You're missing something in your life, and I wager that you're missing that purpose that I mentioned earlier. When you have true purpose in your life, ladies and gentlemen, you will find a peace that you've never known. You will discover how to live as a whole again; not missing pieces, no empty spaces. So I want you to come with me to a new place to find that peace. For those of you willing to take that leap, to find your true potential, there is a bus in back that will take you to our new Eden. You only have to give yourself freely, and the graces will show you the way."

The crowd jumped to its feet with cheers, and Riley joined them. She could see right through the "preacher's" purposefully vague sermon. This wasn't a call to religion. It was delicately crafted propaganda to reach out into the souls of any helpless person, weak people, down on their luck.

Riley finished her soup and followed the masses as most of them lined up outside the tent, alongside a large commercial bus. She recounted Locke's final words to her.

"This will be dangerous, Riley. We won't be able to track you without risking your cover. Once you get on that bus, you'll be on your own."

Riley watched as person after person boarded the bus—a college student, a woman and her baby, an elderly man with a can, and a teenage girl with a hoodie similar to hers. Riley stopped at the door and peered in to see an old man behind the wheel, smiling down at her and inviting her to come in. She continued to recall Locke's message to her.

"We found Samuel Stoke's manifesto. I'm sure the cult has a version of it, themselves. It said that the human race is an albatross to itself. Stoke believes that the fierce among us are fading into oblivion, and humanity was losing its worth. I know that's not true, not completely. You're the proof that he was wrong."

Riley boarded the bus and took her seat as it departed the field and headed out on the open road. Under the pale moonlight, the bus approached a fork in the road and took a left. The sign listed off a bunch of upcoming Texas towns, but at the bottom read *US/MEXICO BORDER*. This is exactly as Locke had predicted it would go. She held onto his words.

"I'm proud of you, Riley. We will find a way to make contact with you once you're down in Panama. We're going to stop them. We're going to stand in their way. I've named our little task force—Albatross Unit."

Riley smiled, and pressed her forehead against the cool glass of the window. The interior lights of the bus shut off and a calming melody played as the group was encourage to get some rest. They had a long journey ahead. Riley took one last glance out the window before closing her eyes.

"Good luck out there, Riley. Be safe."

Joshua D. Howell

ABOUT THE AUTHOR

Joshua D. Howell, out of Omaha, Nebraska, wrote his first novel, Guarding Heaven's Gates, in high school and published it while serving in the military. When he returned to civilian life, he acquired a Bachelor's degree in Legal Studies and has since returned to his writing roots. He has received awards for several works of poetry, and has had a few short stories published in various fiction anthologies. He has a deep passion for the mysteries of science fiction. This novel marks the second book published under the Fierce Literature imprint; the first being the graphic novel adaption of The Fierce Are Fading.

61138690R00142

Made in the USA
Charleston, SC
17 September 2016